PRAISE FOR LAUREN LAYNE

"Exemplary contemporary romance."

—Library Journal

"Flawless contemporary romance—witty, sexy, heartfelt, and hugely entertaining."

—USA TODAY

"The word *charm* is pretty much synonymous with Lauren Layne."

—Hypable

"[A] powerhouse romance author."

—POPSUGAR

Yours to
Keep

Stiletto and Oxford

After the Kiss
Love the One You're With
Just One Night
The Trouble with Love
Irresistibly Yours
I Wish You Were Mine
Someone Like You
I Knew You Were Trouble
I Think I Love You

The Wedding Belles

From This Day Forward (novella)
To Have and to Hold
For Better or Worse
To Love and to Cherish

New York's Finest

Frisk Me
Steal Me
Cuff Me

Redemption

Isn't She Lovely
Broken
Crushed

The Best Mistake

Only with You
Made for You

Yours to Keep

LAUREN LAYNE

Montlake

Published by Montlake, Seattle

www.apub.com

Amazon, the Amazon logo, and Montlake are trademarks of Amazon.com, Inc., or its affiliates.

ISBN-13: 9781542023054
ISBN-10: 154202305X

Cover design by Letitia Hasser

Printed in the United States of America

Chapter One

Carter Ramsey stared at the magazine on his kitchen counter and debated which aspect of his current situation he hated more: The fact that he was drinking his beer with his right hand, because his left arm—his throwing arm—was in a splint. Or the fact that, in a few weeks, his face would be plastered on the front of a magazine in every grocery store and newsstand across the country.

Carter tipped the beer back to his lips and rolled his eyes up to the ceiling. Toss-up. Definitely a toss-up.

He finished the beer and dropped the bottle in the recycling bin as he pulled another out of the fridge, then put it back, annoyed to realize he hadn't really enjoyed the first. Not because he didn't enjoy beer, but because just about every damn thing had tasted bitter in the week since he'd caught Gabe Martinez's line drive mid-air only to feel the unmistakable *snap* in his left arm when he'd fallen to the field moments later.

Plus side? He'd gotten the out.

Downside—and it was a hell of a downside—Carter was on the Injured List for a whopping four to six weeks. Not counting however long rehab took. Not counting the news about his shoulder, which he hadn't even begun to wrap his head around.

One thing he had wrapped his head around? If the New York Hawks—the MLB team Carter had played for during all eight years of his career—made the playoffs, Carter wouldn't be there.

If the Hawks went to the World Series this year, he wouldn't play. And that was *best*-case scenario.

Worst case, he wouldn't accompany the team to the playoffs *any* year, and a lifetime goal of adding a World Series ring to his list of career accomplishments would be dead in the water.

Screw it. Carter pulled the second beer out of the fridge after all, and determinedly opened it using only his right hand. Not because there was anything wrong with his left hand. The fingers worked just fine from where they poked out of the cast. But because using his left side in any capacity only reminded him of how hampered his movements were.

Carter had never been the moody type. He'd never been prone to brooding or male sulking, but *damn*, he was tempted to indulge in a really good wallow right about now. The sort of night that involved fried foods, too much booze, and a woman whose name he probably wouldn't remember in the morning. The sort of night that Carter had rarely indulged in over the years.

One didn't become a six-time All-Star by making bad decisions. But apparently avoiding bad decisions still couldn't prevent him from becoming supermarket tabloid fodder.

Carter took a sip of the beer, then deliberately set the bottle on top of the magazine in front of him, knowing—hoping—that the condensation would warp the glossiness.

Man of the Year.

He shook his head. The title had seemed little more than a nuisance when his agent had called to tell him the "good" news. But actually *seeing* the issue, albeit an early version, was a bitter punch of reality.

Instead of people talking about his Hall of Fame chances, they'd be talking about *this*. A dubious title generally reserved for pretty-boy singers and chiseled-jaw actors headlining the latest action movies. Carter had tried to reassure himself that he was in good company, with last year's winner being the highly respected New York mayor—that the label was an honor.

But right now, with only one working arm and his biggest career dreams teetering on a cliff, it just felt like a mockery.

To be fair, the *Citizen* magazine team behind the Man of the Year issue obviously couldn't have known his injury would coincide with the issue's release, but it was still shitty timing. Carter had skimmed the story only once, but once was enough to know it talked about every glowing aspect of his baseball career: Rookie of the Year, All-Star, American League MVP, Gold Glove, Silver Slugger . . .

There were also several paragraphs on the one accolade that had so far eluded the mighty Carter Ramsey: a World Series ring. Or even a World Series appearance.

As if he needed the reminder. Especially now.

But even that wasn't what was really eating at Carter at the moment. It wasn't what was responsible for his out-of-character brooding, or the slight empty feeling that had been creeping up on him even *before* his injury.

Obnoxiously, it was the *Citizen* mag article that had brought him face-to-face with what was really bothering him: nowhere, in the entire three-page article, was there any mention of who Carter Ramsey was *off* the field. Aside from a few cheeky references to his love life and penchant for dating models, there was nothing to tell the world who Carter was when his hand wasn't in a baseball glove, or when he wasn't showcasing the "model swing" that had once been written up in *Physics Today*.

Carter already knew he was a good ball player—maybe even an exceptional one. After this magazine came out, non–baseball fans would know it, too.

But with his arm in a sling and his name off the Hawks' active roster . . .

Who the hell was he?

And where did he belong?

1

Nobody wanted to know as much as Carter himself. He was rich, successful, and revered, yes. And it was fantastic. He was also single, not getting any younger . . . and a little bit lonely.

He picked up his beer, taking one last look down at his own face grinning out from beneath the Hawks cap on the cover, then flipped the magazine over in disgust. Then he cursed once more when he saw his face again, this time on an ad, showing off the luxury watch brand he endorsed.

Empty bullshit.

Irritably, Carter turned his attention from the magazine to his phone, and wandered over to the floor-to-ceiling windows of his Manhattan apartment. He was oblivious to the Empire State Building view as he scrolled through his contacts, debating how to fill the time. Carter had always been a social guy. He was the likable athlete who hosted fundraisers instead of avoiding them, the guy who was always down for a pickup game of basketball or a spontaneous night on the town with new friends, or old.

Now, he was faced with the hard realization that his core social circle was his team. Most of his go-to grab-a-beer or workout buddies were in Houston, warming up for tonight's game against the Astros, which Carter fully expected them to win.

Not that he'd bring himself to watch the game. He'd kept up on the Hawks in the days since his injury, in that he checked their standing in the league religiously. Partially out of loyalty to the team as well as for genuine interest in his friends' careers. But knowing Roy Denizen was at shortstop instead of himself and having to *watch* Roy take his spot on the field were two different things entirely.

As Carter grew more restless by the minute, his thumb continued to scroll through the names, and he told himself to just pick someone at random. It didn't really matter who. Anyone would be better than hanging home alone, moping. He needed to be around people, needed to ease the antsy feeling he got whenever he wasn't on the field.

He paused on Laura's name, a sort of on-again-off-again fling who didn't take life too seriously, and didn't give him grief when they often went months between "meetings."

She seemed to enjoy his company, she didn't drive him nuts. *Good enough.*

He'd started to text Laura when his phone buzzed with an incoming call.

Carter's communication was ruled almost entirely by text messages, but there were a few exceptions. His sixty-year-old agent. His old-school manager. His fiftysomething parents. And strangely, his sister, who despite being his twin, and thus the exact same age as twenty-eight-year-old Carter, was apparently in a pre-Y2K time warp, because she vastly preferred talking on the phone over texting.

Still. It was his *twin.*

So he answered the phone with a smile. "Sister."

"Brother! You picked up!"

"You sound surprised."

"Well, yeah. You *never* pick up."

"Hyperbole. It's just that you usually call when I'm at practice or at a game." He retrieved his beer from the kitchen as he talked, then dropped onto his couch. "But turns out I've got some free time on my hands these days."

"Hands? Or hand?"

He snorted in spite of his bad mood, and his sister sighed in relief. "Oh thank God. I was worried it was too soon for jokes."

"Since when has that stopped you?"

"Good point. But I'm my brother's sister. Humor's how we cope."

True enough. Caitlyn was more or less a female version of himself. Competitive, but in a deceptively laid-back, sneak-up-on-you kind of way. Both had inherited their mother's cheerful extroversion, their father's sharp sense of humor. Carter didn't see his twin as often as he liked, but Caitlyn was one of the few people on the planet guaranteed never to kiss his ass or walk on eggshells around him. Exactly what he needed right now.

"So, rumor has it I'll be seeing your face at Walmart next month," she said in a casual tone.

His eyes narrowed in suspicion. "Oh yeah?"

"Mom told me the good news. Man of the Year," she said in a mocking hushed, deferential tone. "Does that come with a ring that I should kiss when I'm blessed by your presence? Also, please tell me they Photoshopped your ugly face. No *way* do I have that many more eye wrinkles than you when you're four minutes older."

"How did you even see the damn thing?" Carter asked. "It's not supposed to hit newsstands until September."

"Dan mailed an early version of the cover to Mom."

Of course. Carter pressed the cold bottle to his forehead and closed his eyes and made a mental note: never introduce one's longtime agent to one's mother, especially when they shared an affinity for *The West Wing*, peanut butter on waffles, and *knowing all things about Carter Ramsey's life.*

"Mom tore out all of the pages from your story, plus that weird watch ad, and taped them to her fridge," Caitlyn continued. "But not before I snagged the cover page, and held it up to my enormous stomach. The way I see it, that magazine is the only way Unborn is going to be able to recognize her uncle."

In spite of his ragged mood, Carter smiled at the thought of his sister becoming a mom—he'd been thrilled for Caitlyn and AJ the moment he'd heard they were expecting. He was still thrilled. He couldn't wait to be an uncle.

And yet, an uncomfortable feeling settled between his shoulder blades at the realization that, given his schedule, he was unlikely to see his niece or nephew aside from Thanksgiving or Christmas. Even more bittersweet was the reminder that he had no family of his own, and quite honestly, he'd really thought he'd have one by now. If not kids, at least a wife. Instead, the closest he had was a series of one-night stands with Laura, whose last name he was blanking on.

Carter laughed to push away the dark thoughts. "Well, this is a thrilling bonus to your pregnancy. A new way to guilt me."

"Yes, for sure," she said sarcastically. "AJ and I were on the fence about starting a family, but then we're like, 'You know what, this would make such a great Carter guilt trip, let's do it . . .'"

"You could have saved yourself the morning sickness," Carter said. "I already got the guilt trip from Mom earlier today. And wait, back up. What did you mean, you held the cover up to your stomach? You just stick my face in front of your pregnant belly? I'm uncomfortable."

"Would it be better if I told you I made AJ read it aloud and pretend to be you? It was a lot about RBIs and batting averages, but I think Unborn dug it."

"Disturbing," he replied. "And it reminds me, I've been meaning to call the Vatican and ask how that nomination for your husband into sainthood is coming along."

"Please," she said with a scoff. "I'm six months pregnant and still manage to make AJ his favorite blueberry pie every Friday, so when the pope finally does answer your call, you can go ahead and mention *that* to His Holiness. Also, while you've got him on the line, see if you can squeeze in a confession."

"For?"

"For going eight months since your last visit home."

He grimaced. "I think you missed the part where I said Mom already guilt-tripped me today."

"It's been since *Christmas*, Carter. Normally, I get it. The schedule of a pro baseball player is no joke, but now that you're . . ."

"Now that I'm on the Injured List and out of the game?" he finished for her.

A longer-than-usual moment passed before she replied, her tone slightly gentler. "Yeah. That. You know I'm super bummed for you. It seriously sucks. But since you've got the time off, why not come home? It's only a couple hours' drive, and we'd love to see you. Like, I'd really, really love it."

Carter slowly blew out a breath, and rode the wave of guilt. His twin was right. He wasn't great about getting back to Haven regularly, preferring to host his parents here in the city whenever possible. Not because he had any particular beef or baggage related to his hometown—it was just a little sedate compared to his usual lifestyle.

Carter glanced down at his sling. *Chill* was on his agenda for the next month or so, anyway. Why not get in some face time with the fam . . .

"And," Caitlyn went on, "I'm cochairing our ten-year high school reunion. I know you said you had a game and couldn't go, but that was before."

All optimistic thoughts about Haven fled. It was one thing to think about catching up with his parents, maybe finally getting around to watching *Game of Thrones*, or *Breaking Bad*, or any number of TV shows he'd been missing out on. But a cheesy high school reunion?

A flippant *no thanks* was already on the tip of his tongue, but Carter bit it back at the last second, suddenly seeing himself from his sister's perspective and not liking what he saw.

When had he become *that* guy? The hotshot celeb who was too busy and important to give a single evening of his life to the people who'd had his back all throughout his teen years? Especially since it wasn't as though he had a big tragic backstory. Carter had had an exceptionally happy childhood, with a loving, supportive family, raised in a quirky small town that, while hardly cosmopolitan, had been a damn fine place to grow up.

Still. A high school reunion? He was again hit by visions of a punch bowl, disco ball, retro music . . .

Carter was a good guy, not a martyr.

"I thought the reunion wasn't until Labor Day?" he asked, pleased that he remembered their last conversation, when she'd mentioned that Haven High's ten-year reunions always fell on Labor Day weekend.

"It's not, but already, everyone is rolling their eyes whenever it gets mentioned," she huffed.

"Shocking," he muttered.

"See, that attitude is exactly the problem," she said. "Everyone is playing like they're too cool for a dorky reunion."

"Wow, you're really selling it."

"So I was thinking," she continued as though he hadn't spoken. "In order to get people to come, I need to make it cool, and I can think of two ways to do that."

"Cancel it and postpone indefinitely?" he proposed.

"I was thinking more along the lines of a celebrity cameo!"

"I'm sure Taylor Swift would clear her entire schedule," Carter replied.

"Come on!" she said, with her trademark Caitlyn impatience. "You know people will show up if they hear you'll be there. Whenever you do come to town, it's only for a couple days and you never leave Mom and Dad's. Hardly anyone's even seen you since high school, Carter. Other than Jakey, you don't keep in touch with people."

Guilt flared again, because she was right. He'd never meant to be that guy who'd left his supportive hometown and barely looked back; it had just sort of . . . happened. Even when he wasn't constantly on the road—and he usually was—his lifestyle now made the distance between Haven and Manhattan seem a lot farther than the two-hour drive.

Still, he deflected. "Using your brother's career to get people to the reunion? You're better than that."

"I'm really not," Caitlyn said. "And I get it, a high school reunion is the equivalent of a terrible made-for-TV movie, but . . ."

He waited, then rolled his eyes to the ceiling when she didn't finish her sentence. "Go ahead. Lay your closing argument on me."

"Trust me, I'm dying to. But Mom told me not to get involved in your personal life," she said hesitantly.

His eyebrows went up. "Really? Because just a few hours ago I listened to her tell me her theories on the relationship between jock straps and male infertility."

"Don't be gross."

"Don't be cagey. Spit it out."

"Let's just say hypothetically, if I could think of a really enticing reason why you might want to come back . . ."

"I *will* hang up on you," he replied, patience unraveling at his sister's hedging.

"I keep hearing that Felicity's coming back to town," she blurted out.

Carter went still, a rush of memories washing over him. "Felicity?"

"Uh-huh. Remember her? The girl you were head-over-heels with in high school? The one everyone thought you were going to marry?"

Carter let out a strangled laugh, because his sister didn't know the half of it. His childish pact with his high school girlfriend was just about the only secret he'd kept from Caitlyn over the years. A secret he'd kept from *everyone*, because in hindsight, it was damned ridiculous. Not to mention, it had become irrelevant the moment he'd heard Felicity had moved to LA and married some hotshot Hollywood director.

"That's your big pitch?" he asked. "Me hanging out with my ex from ten years ago and her husband? Easy *nope*."

"She doesn't have a husband," Caitlyn said.

Carter's beer froze halfway to his lips. "What?"

"She's not married anymore. Her divorce was finalized a couple months ago. She's single . . . You're single . . ."

Carter slowly sat up straight, setting his beer on the table. Now, that was interesting.

Very interesting indeed.

Suddenly, Carter was presented with a different version of his life. A different path, had he made different choices. And he knew do-overs weren't a thing. Not usually.

But then people didn't usually do what he and Felicity George had done ten years ago.

"Well played, Cait," he told his sister distractedly. "You just got yourself a good old-fashioned homecoming."

Chapter Two

"Son of a—"

The fact that she snapped her mouth shut before finishing the oath was as much a function of the glitter as it was years of practice biting her tongue in front of her students before a "swear," as her boss liked to call them, slipped out.

Eyes squeezed shut, lips clamped together, Olive Dunn stood perfectly still to endure the cloud of green glitter currently seeping into her pores, praying that when it was over, the results would be worth it.

Finally, she opened her eyes and glanced down. And sighed. Not worth it.

That perky Martha Stewart wannabe on YouTube had made it look deceptively easy. But what was supposed to be a lion perfectly outlined with green glitter on the black poster board more closely resembled Slimer from *Ghostbusters*. Granted, Olive had always been sort of a fan of Slimer. But he wasn't the mascot of Haven High. Pity.

"Dahm," Olive said vehemently, mouth full of glitter. She still had a solid month before the school year started up—might as well get the "swears" out of her system now.

The curse was not without penalty. She coughed as a fresh batch of glitter particles got into her mouth, tickling the back of her throat. Still hacking, she headed to the counter and grabbed a paper towel, swiping futilely at the glitter coating her tongue.

"Dahm, dahm, dahm," she repeated. If one were going to give in to a vice, one might as well do it with gusto.

Olive tossed the paper towel in the recycling and poured a glass of water. She swished it around in her mouth as she glared at the ill-fated art project on her kitchen table.

There went her Pinterest cred.

She'd always preferred science labs to art classes, and apparently, not much had changed in the decade since she'd graduated high school. Honestly, the fact that the glitter covered most of the poster board was a bit of a blessing. It disguised the fact she'd attempted to write "10 years!" in fancy block letters, the exclamation point sporting a distinct cock-and-balls vibe.

Which, come to think of it, was the closest she'd gotten to male genitalia in way too long.

Olive continued to swish as she tilted her head and studied the poster. Maybe the poster resembling boy parts wouldn't have been such a bad thing. A penis poster was probably the most thrilling thing about Haven High's upcoming ten-year reunion.

She still wasn't exactly sure how she'd gotten pulled in last minute to help cochair. In fact, she'd been unenthused about even attending, much less hosting. Not because high school held bad memories or threatened to unearth dark secrets worthy of a Netflix miniseries. It was just that when you had a middling high school experience and lived in the same small town where most of your graduating class also still lived, a reunion seemed a bit redundant. She could see like half her sophomore geometry class just by going to Walgreens for Pepto-Bismol.

Alas, sometime in the past few years, she'd found herself becoming close friends with their senior class president, and it turned out saying no to a pregnant Caitlyn Cortez was pretty much impossible. Especially when her friend had pleaded swollen ankles and pregnancy brain. Neither were things Olive had personal experience with, but she *did* love to be in charge of stuff. Plus, Olive was a high school teacher at the same school she'd graduated. School spirit was sort of part of the job description.

And so, here she was, full of glitter.

Olive leaned over the sink and spit green. She set the water glass aside and bent to pull a garbage bag out from under the sink, since she was relatively sure the poster board was no longer recyclable after her sparkly addition. She shook open the bag with a *snap*, wondering about the best way to approach glitter cleanup. Was there a special glitter vacuum? Some sort of magic potion?

Olive made a mental note to text Kelly and ask.

She and Kelly Byrne—now Kelly Blakely—hadn't been close growing up. But then, Olive hadn't been close with *anyone* growing up. Kelly had graduated a couple of years ahead of her, and Olive had not exactly been the type of sophomore that seniors brought into their inner circle, even friendly seniors like Kelly had been.

But last year, they'd been assigned as roommates at a Hudson Valley teacher conference, and they'd become fast friends. And most crucially of all, Kelly taught elementary school and was thus nearly fluent in glitter, unlike Olive's high school biology teacher self.

The sound of a car and movement outside her window caught Olive's attention, and all thoughts of glitter and Kelly and penis-shaped exclamation points faded.

Olive lived on the very outskirts of Haven, which meant aside from the vacant home next door, she had no neighbors. She liked it that way. Nobody to see her ABBA dance parties, or to discover that she had names for every single one of the crows that gathered in her yard every winter morning to eat the bread she bought specifically for them.

But it also meant that traffic of any kind was unusual.

She went to the window and narrowed her eyes as a black car pulled up to the curb outside the vacant neighboring house. The car was sleek and new, a sedan the likes of which wealthy, possibly scarred movie villains were driven around in.

The owners? Olive wondered. She'd never met them. Rumor had it a swanky Manhattan couple had bought the house as an escape from the city, but one of them had gotten a job transfer to London, and they'd never bothered to sell their Haven escape house.

Other than a maintenance crew that came by once a month to mow the lawn, run water through the pipes, and check for rodents or whatever, it had been more or less abandoned the entire three years Olive had lived next door.

The driver's door opened, and an honest-to-God chauffeur climbed out, with the uniform and hat and everything. The driver reached for the handle of the back passenger door, which the passenger pushed open.

Olive's eyes narrowed even further as a long—very long—denim-clad leg stepped out of the car.

That leg was not from around here.

She watched as the man said something to the driver, then slammed the car door shut, looking up at the house through shade-covered eyes.

Everything about him seemed vaguely expensive. He was wearing jeans, yes, but they seemed to be the *cost more than Olive's car payment* variety. The black T-shirt was too sleek and well fitted to be from Walmart, and flattered a *very* impressive male form. The only thing marring the perfection was a sling holding his left arm immobile. Vaguely intriguing. Probably a yachting injury. That was a thing, right?

Olive's eyebrows lifted as the chauffeur went to the trunk of the car and pulled out a sleek-looking silver roller bag and a black duffel. Enough luggage to mean that Mr. Injured Fancy was staying, at least for a little while.

That made the situation go from vaguely intriguing to need-to-know.

He may own the house, but this was *her* turf, and in Haven, it was simply not acceptable for strangers to remain strangers, especially when he was a man alone next to a woman alone, and she hadn't had a chance to assess his Creep and Douche levels.

Best to do so now, when the chauffeur could serve as witness if he tried to murder her.

Olive pulled away from the window and went shooting out her front door and across her front lawn. "Excuse me. Sir?"

The man slowly turned toward her, but with the sunglasses and New York Hawks ball cap shading his face, she didn't get a better sense of him head-on than she had from his profile.

Except that the closer she got, the more masculine he seemed.

Olive was five ten, and not the waifish model type of five ten, but a solid, *I come from Viking stock* type of five ten. Very few people could make her feel petite.

This man did.

"Hi," she said, slightly out of breath from her spontaneous dash across their yards. "I live next door. And you are?"

He didn't have to remove his aviator glasses for her to know he was giving her a slow once-over, his head tilting to the side. "Olive? Olive Dunn?"

That she had not been expecting. "Have we met?"

"I'd say so."

He reached out and removed his sunglasses at the same moment a smile broke over his face. An irritatingly familiar smile, one she hadn't seen in person for ten years, but one you couldn't avoid seeing on the television anytime the New York Hawks were playing.

Haven's golden boy had returned.

"Oh, hell," she muttered.

He let out a surprised laugh. "Nice way to greet your old lab partner."

"I'm surprised you even recognized me," Olive muttered.

"Why wouldn't I recognize you?"

The comment wasn't meant as an insult. There was no jab in his tone, his expression more puzzled than cruel. But it stung all the same. And it irritated her that it stung. It irritated Olive that there was some tiny, ridiculous part of her that still clung to her "swan" fantasies, where the awkward teen turned into the stunningly beautiful woman, where coworkers at her swanky new job would look at pictures of her nerdy teen self with a gasp. *No! That can't be you!*

But that wasn't Olive's story. It was never going to be Olive's story. She'd been too big, too loud, too weird in high school. And she was too big, too loud, and too weird now.

As for him, Carter Ramsey was the boy swan who'd turned into an even more beautiful man swan. He'd been popular and good-looking in high school, and now he was professional baseball's MVP and highest-paid player.

She didn't want to say it was unfair, because no doubt he'd worked hard, but it was definitely aggravating.

"Well, well, well," she said, crossing her arms and studying him. "What brings you back to Haven? Did they name a street after you or something?"

They hadn't. She'd know. But she wouldn't be the least bit surprised if it happened in her lifetime.

He lifted the cast-covered left arm as much as he could, given the constraints of the sling. She noticed a tattoo on the sliver of skin peeking between the end of his T-shirt sleeve and the top of the sling. It was hot. Damn it. "I've got a few days off."

"Not by choice, I'm guessing, based on your sour expression?"

"Good guess, Dunn. You correctly deduced that I did not, in fact, plan to break my arm and spend the most crucial part of the regular season off the field, putzing around my hometown."

"Ooh. Sensitive topic," she said.

"You think?" he snapped.

She couldn't help her grin. "Interesting. So you *have* changed."

"Meaning?"

"The Carter I remember couldn't go thirty seconds without smiling and charming everyone in his path. This one, though . . ." She waved her hand over him. "Let's just say I'm not charmed."

Except, if she were being honest with herself, she was. A little.

Perfect high school Carter hadn't appealed to her in the least. Yes, he'd been good-looking, and to be fair, he'd been a nice enough guy, albeit a little self-absorbed with his own athletic glory. All in all, he'd been perfect at the expense of being interesting.

This Carter, though . . .

She studied him more closely. All the good looks were still there, but there was just the slightest edge about him. That tattoo alone signaled that the squeaky-clean Carter she remembered had grown up a bit. But it was more than ink on his arm—there were internal changes, too. Simple age and maturity, perhaps? Or resentment of his injury? Whatever the cause, she sensed a slight depth to him now that bumped his attractiveness up several notches, as far as she was concerned.

"From what I remember, you were impossible to charm," Carter groused, unaware of her thoughts.

She snorted. "Right. Because you spent so much time trying to win me over. Clearly, I'd have fit right in with the rest of your harem."

Though, to be fair, toward the end of their senior year, there hadn't been a harem. Just one girl. Another of the *Beautiful People*, who, rumor had it, was recently single and making her way back to Haven.

"Oh gawd," she said on a groan. "Don't tell me. Our prodigal prom king and queen are headed for a reconciliation just in time for my reunion."

"*Your* reunion? I seem to remember there were nearly a hundred of us in the graduating class."

"I'm chairing it. Well, cochairing it with—your sister," she said, belatedly remembering that Caitlyn Cortez was previously Caitlyn Ramsey, Carter's twin.

15

"Oh that's right. I think she mentioned that. What she didn't mention was that the house she found for me to rent was next door to yours."

"Now that you know, any chance you'll . . ." She used her index and middle finger to indicate he should scamper off to wherever he'd come from. "I rather like my isolation."

She didn't mean to be rude, but she really *did* prefer her solitude. Olive was talkative, outgoing, and she loved her town and the people in it. But she was an introvert at heart—it was why she'd opted to live out here, away from the main part of town. She loved being able to be a part of the bustle when it suited her, but also have a retreat from people to think.

"Nah, I think I'll stay," he said with an easy grin. "From what I remember, we got along pretty well, right?"

"If by 'got along' you mean that I aced every single lab assignment while you couldn't even identify a beaker from a Bunsen burner."

Okay, that was petty.

And not entirely fair. Carter may have been a jock, but he hadn't been the cliché stupid version from teen movies. Still, she definitely remembered him being a lot more interested in sneaking looks at his cell phone when Mr. Witte's back had been turned than he had been in taking notes.

"It's good to see you again, Olive," Carter said with a friendly grin, fishing a set of keys out of his jeans pocket. "Or should I say, *neighbor.*"

He turned and jogged up the stepped walkway to the front steps, and Olive nearly charged after him to demand an explanation of how long he intended to be in town, as well as share her thoughts on loud music after nine p.m., when a pointed throat-clearing to her right caught her attention.

She turned to the chauffeur. The middle-aged man was solemnly holding out a pristine white handkerchief toward her.

Olive gave it a puzzled look, then glanced up at the driver. "What's that for?"

He merely cleared his throat again, and though his implacable expression never changed, his eyes flicked, not quite rudely, but pointedly, all the way down to her feet and then all the way back up, ending with his gaze on her hairline. He gave the handkerchief a meaningful shake. *You really need this.*

"I don't—"

Olive groaned as realization sank in.

Haven's illustrious golden boy was back in town. And she had just welcomed him while covered head to toe in green glitter.

Chapter Three

Carter was smiling as he tossed the keys on the kitchen counter and dropped his bag onto the hardwood floors.

Olive Dunn.

His chemistry lab partner from senior year hadn't changed a bit. Granted, the green, sparkly look was new. The Olive he remembered had been far more into copper chloride than kindergarten-variety glitter.

But her strange appearance had been the perfect welcome home. A refreshing change from his neighbors on the Upper East Side, who wouldn't dream of having a hair out of place, much less dressing up as a leprechaun, or whatever Olive Dunn was about these days.

People weren't afraid to be themselves in Haven, and Olive had always flown her quirky flag especially high and proud. He'd liked that about her, so he hadn't uttered a word about her appearance just now, not even a cheesy pun about her being olive green.

Live and let live, as his mother always said.

A knock pounded at the front door. A second later it burst open, and a blur of blonde and green sparkles marched into his kitchen. Behind Olive, Carter saw Mike hovering in the doorway with the luggage. Carter nodded in thanks as the chauffeur left his bags just inside the front door. He liked Mike well enough, but he was also eager for the man to leave. Being delivered to your hometown, just two hours north of your current home, felt like a douchebag move. A broken arm didn't preclude him from driving himself. But the team's coordinator had insisted, probably to make Carter feel like he was "still part of the team."

At least the only person who'd seen him riding into town like a prima donna was Olive, who was now roaming around his kitchen.

He turned his attention to the green interloper. "Did you just let yourself into my house?"

Olive unapologetically inspected the appliances and tile backsplash before turning to face him.

"Well, you should have locked the door if you didn't want company," she said pragmatically.

"Oh, sorry. I didn't realize that coming uninvited into someone's house was a thing that people actually did."

She shrugged as she opened his microwave, then closed it again. "You obviously don't remember life in Haven all that well. An open-door policy is sort of small-town MO. Also, I have this same microwave." She pointed at the countertop appliance. "It looks fancy, but don't use the popcorn button unless you want to set off the smoke detector and prefer your popcorn to taste like burned dust. Though it does do a really nice job with baked potatoes."

"I thought you liked your solitude?" he asked, bemused.

"Given the choice, sure. But since you're here . . ." Olive hoisted herself into a seated position on the counter beside his kitchen sink. "So, you're renting this place?"

It was part question, part demand, as though it were her right to know his every bit of business, but since he had no reason not to tell her, he shrugged. "I subleased it from the owners through September."

She whistled. "Almost two months. That's got to be a record for you, right? Last time you were in town was Christmas, and you stayed for . . . two days?"

Some of his easygoing amusement faded. "Were we closer friends than I remember? You seem awfully interested in my business."

"Not your business. *Everyone's* business. I'm what some might call a busybody." She grinned as she said it, and though she'd wiped some of the glitter off her face between the car and barging into his kitchen, her features were still mostly green, making her teeth look extremely white in contrast.

He found himself smiling back, in spite of his irritation with her. He didn't remember Olive the teenager being particularly smiley. At least not in the sweet, charming way that Felicity and some of the more popular girls had been. Olive had been more focused on *doing* things than smiling about them.

But when she did smile, it was an all-out grin, unapologetic, endearing, and damn hard not to respond to.

"So this is a thing you do then? Let yourself into other people's houses and interrogate them?" he asked.

"If there's a need." She hopped down and opened his fridge. "You'll need to do a grocery run."

"Yeah. I was planning to hit up Turner & Reed this afternoon for some basics," he said, referring to one of the local grocery stores in town.

"Turner & Reed?" she said, closing the door and turning toward him.

"Are they not open anymore?" he said, feeling a little chagrined that he'd been gone so long he didn't even know where to buy food in his hometown.

"Oh no, they're open," she said. "And doing great. Jennie Reed took it over from her parents a while back and it's even fancier than it was before. Truffle-flavored everything."

"So what's the problem?" he asked.

"It's just not the place you go for basics unless you want to pay six dollars for a carton of eggs." He stared at her for a moment, and she laughed. "You have no idea if that's expensive or not, do you?"

Carter gave a sheepish grin. "I confess it's been a few years since I bought my own groceries."

Olive's eyebrows lifted. "Have you *ever* had to buy your groceries?"

He merely smiled wider.

Olive sighed. "I know you probably have more money than every person in this town combined, but I can't let you do this." She stepped forward and picked up the iPhone on the counter.

"That's mine," Carter said.

"I know." She held it up, screen facing out in front of his face, and used the facial recognition to unlock it.

"*Busybody* does not even begin to describe you," he said under his breath.

"Heard that," she said, not looking up from his phone.

"You were supposed to."

She said nothing for a moment longer, thumbs busy, then handed his phone back. "Ta-da."

Carter took it reluctantly and glanced down to see his Maps app open. "What am I looking at?"

"Directions to Walmart. *That's* where you should buy your groceries."

"I can't believe Haven has a Walmart now," he mused, zooming in on the screen to see where in his small town they'd fit the behemoth superstore, annoyed that he had to set the phone on the counter in order to do so with his one free hand.

"Heck yes we have a Walmart. It's about a fifteen-minute drive, and I feel like I should warn you that you'll stand out like a sore thumb when your fancy driver takes you there."

"Mike's already on his way back to the city," Carter said.

"What? He doesn't say goodbye? *You* don't say goodbye?"

"Trust me, Mike likes it that way. On the talkative scale, there's you." He extended his free hand all the way outward. "And if this other arm weren't in a cast, imagine me spreading my arm as far as it could go the other way. That's where Mike is on the scale. Practically a mute. The cast, admittedly, weakens the visual effect."

She stepped closer to him and extended her right arm out to the side, to where his casted left arm couldn't. "There. An assist."

"Thanks," he said with a laugh, realizing it had been a long time since he'd spent time with someone like Olive Dunn. In fact, it had been ten years, since they'd been lab partners, because there was no one else like her.

Her gaze dropped to his cast. "How long do you have to wear that thing?"

"Four to six weeks. Hopefully." He braced himself for one of the pitying *oh no* looks he'd been getting nonstop over the past week. No matter how many times Carter reminded himself that it was compassion, it was getting increasingly tiresome to have people look at him like his life was over just because his career had hit a pothole.

Instead of a pitying look, Olive reached out and flicked the cast gently, experimentally, then simply said, "Huh. Well, good seeing you again, I suppose."

She stepped back and headed toward his front door, apparently planning to exit as unceremoniously as she'd entered; then she turned back. "Hey, wait. If your driver's gone, how will you get around? You should have rented a place closer to Franklin Street. The only thing within walking distance from here is my house."

"Lucky me," he said with a small smile. "And I'm picking up a car from Billy's later."

"Picking up a car from Billy's—as in, Billy's Dealership?"

"Yup."

She blinked. "I didn't realize he did rentals."

Carter smiled again.

She sighed. "You're going to buy a car, aren't you? Just for the month or so you're going to be here?"

"Say, that reminds me. Do you know anyone who'd want to buy a like-new car in four to six weeks?"

She rolled her eyes and walked out of his kitchen and disappeared, only to stick her head back in at the last moment. "Of course I do. We'll talk when it gets closer." Olive disappeared again, and the kitchen turned silent—too silent.

He followed her as she opened his front door. "Where are you going?" he asked.

"To shower, obviously. I can't drive you to Billy's looking like this," she said, gesturing with both hands over her green-glitter body.

For the first time, Carter registered that the legs beneath the glitter were long, strong, and very shapely. "You're driving me to Billy's?"

"Of course. How else would you get there?" she said, as though this were very clear, and he were very slow. "Wheels up in fifteen, Baseball. Don't make me wait." She stepped out onto his front porch and shut the door.

Only after he saw a green, sparkly blur shoot across the lawn to the house next door did he fully absorb what had happened.

He had just been yanked back into small-town life by an admittedly strange source, and . . . he didn't hate it.

"See, now I think this plan is coming along really nicely, don't you?" Olive asked, looking across the console of her secondhand car at Carter with a grin.

"What plan? The one where you kidnap me?"

"Please. You're too big for such things, and you got into my car quite willingly," she pointed out.

"Only because you're taking me to pick up my new car, ensuring I have a mode of transportation should I need to escape my crazy new neighbor."

"Speaking of that, can you drive with one arm?" Olive asked.

Carter looked pointedly across the car at where she had her right hand on the wheel, her left elbow propped on the open window, her fingers spread as she let the air rush through them.

"Fair point," Olive acknowledged. "Still, it must suck."

"Having a broken arm? A little bit." He turned and looked out the window. His aviator glasses were back in place, and Olive got the distinct impression that he wore them as much to hide his mood as he did against the August sunshine. Not because Carter Ramsey was a moody kind of guy—quite the opposite, he seemed rather likable. But it didn't take a genius to see that his current state frustrated him.

"Being dependent on people to help you is annoying," she said sympathetically.

"What?" He looked back toward her. "Oh. Yeah. Though that's not the worst part. It's more not being able to do the thing I love most in the world."

"Oh, you mean . . ." She made a crude gesture with her hand, and Carter let out a surprised laugh and shook his head.

"Not that," he said.

"Ah. That thing you do with the other stick and balls," she said.

Instead of replying he turned more fully toward her. "Wait, back up. What plan is going along 'really nicely'?" He lifted his good hand to make air quotes as he said it.

"My plan to make you a nonstranger."

"When did you hatch this plan?"

"The second I saw your car drive up and assumed you were the hotshot owner of the house next door who'd finally decided to grace Haven with your presence. Then, of course, I realized you were a hotshot *renter* of the house who finally decided to grace Haven with your presence, but the plan stayed the same."

"What, to harass me?"

"Nope. To eliminate all stranger-danger vibes."

"You know me from high school. How am I a stranger?"

"I *knew* you from high school, past tense. People change," she said.

"You haven't." The way he muttered it made her think it wasn't a compliment, but she understood that she was an acquired taste.

"I suppose you haven't much, either," she admitted. "Still annoyingly good-looking, with a touch of ego, and big legs."

"Big legs?" he echoed.

"You know. Sporty legs. Strong." She reached across to pat his thigh, but he caught her hand and placed it purposely on her own leg.

"Yours aren't so bad, either," he said.

"Right?" She beamed proudly. "Arms are my favorite workout—I love the fast results. But I've been giving my lower body some love at the gym this year and it's finally paying off."

"Indeed," he said noncommittally.

"Here we are!" she said, turning into Billy's parking lot and pulling up into one of the spots. "Which one's yours?"

"Guess I'm about to find out," he said, unbuckling his seat belt.

"You don't know?" she said, aghast.

"It's only for a few weeks. Don't really care."

"Oh, but you must care." She unbuckled her own seat belt. "Here, I'll come help. I know Billy."

"Of course you do," he said with a sigh, but he smiled this time, and he seemed more resigned than annoyed.

"See? Plan coming along nicely."

Chapter Four

Once out of Olive's car, Carter turned and lifted a hand, intending to wave farewell to his amusing, if slightly exhausting, new neighbor, and tell her that while her offer was appreciated, he really could manage to buy a car without her supervision.

Carter hadn't seen Olive in ten years, had spent all of thirty minutes in her company this decade. He couldn't claim to know her well.

But she was already out of the car, shoving her keys into her back pocket.

Carter's hand dropped with a sigh. "There's no chance I can politely decline your help, is there?"

"You said that you hadn't bought groceries yourself in like ever. Car shopping is *way* trickier than buying eggs. I can't, in good conscience, let a pampered celebrity like yourself get taken advantage of. Billy's the best, but he's also smart and will be able to spot a sucker."

"Pampered celebrity? Wait . . . sucker?" he called after her, following Olive into the small office building.

Billy's Dealership looked pretty much like it had when Carter's parents had brought Caitlyn and him on their sixteenth birthday to pick a used car to share. There were the same brightly colored red balloons tied to the handwritten sign in the driveway—the bouquet small, but cheerful. Same assortment of shiny new Hondas and not-so-shiny Cadillacs older than Carter.

Though, if he wasn't mistaken, the enormous "Billy's" sign and logo were new, even if the building beneath them was not. Thankfully, the old building had top-notch air-conditioning, and Carter relished the blast of cold air as he stepped inside behind Olive.

The bell on the door tinkled as they entered, and almost immediately, an older woman wearing a flowy bright pink dress with even brighter yellow flowers printed on it emerged. Her hair was short and purple in color. Everything about her was bright, and Carter blinked, suddenly tempted to put his sunglasses back on just to look at her.

"Olive, darling, what are you—" The woman broke off as she fixed her attention on Carter. "Carter Ramsey, is that you?"

"Please," Olive answered for him in a dismissive tone. "Of course it's him. He's one of a kind. God and the angels had to retire his model after Carter was born because Earth could only handle so much glory."

Carter had time for only the briefest of *hu ha* looks in Olive's direction before the older woman was coming toward him, giving him an honest-to-God cheek squeeze. "I haven't seen you since you were . . ." She started to lift her hand to indicate his height, then dropped it. "Well, I guess you were already about this tall the last time I saw you. But still, you're all grown up!"

Carter felt a surge of panic. He had no idea who this woman was.

Olive spoke up. "Carter, of course you remember Mona. She's been working at Billy's almost since he opened the place."

Carter blinked in surprise. Mona? The only Mona he remembered was Mona Pullen, the diminutive, *blend in with the wall* receptionist who he vaguely remembered processing the paperwork for his and Caitlyn's first Camry purchase all those years ago. Looking closer, he saw it was that Mona, just with a whole new look and attitude.

He shot Olive a brief thank-you smile for the name assist before grinning at the older woman. "Mona. Of course I recognized you, but barely. Are you aging in reverse?"

Mona gave a girlish giggle that had Olive rolling her eyes. "I *do* feel younger after Olive here helped give me a makeover a few years ago."

Ah. Suddenly, Mona's appearance made a lot more sense. The brightly colored everything *would* be the handiwork of a woman who, less than an hour ago, had been covered in green glitter.

"Well, we had to do something to bring Billy to his senses, didn't we?" Olive said.

"My ears are burning," a man said, coming out of the back office even as he shoved a cell phone into his pocket.

"Just remembering the dark days before you made an honest woman out of Mona," Olive said, patting the man fondly on the back.

Not just a makeover artist then, Carter thought. Olive was also a matchmaker. He was rapidly gathering that they were likely just a couple of the many hats this woman wore in Haven.

"Dark days indeed," Billy said, gazing adoringly at Mona before shifting his attention back to Olive and Carter. "Sorry about the delay. I was on the phone with the big fancy bank I just joined, and it took me nearly twenty minutes of shouting at a machine just to get to a damn person. Now what can I—"

He broke off when he seemed to finally register Carter's presence. Not that it was surprising. Carter may be a head taller than everyone in the room, and famous, but it was hard to compete with the likes of Olive Dunn and Mona Pullen.

"Well, hot damn," Billy said, striding over to Carter with a grin. "Carter Ramsey, good to see you, son!"

Carter extended his hand for a hearty shake, smiling at the man, whose voice and overall persona were every bit as booming now as they had been when he'd taken Carter and Caitlyn on a generous number of test drives twelve years ago.

Billy had definite shades of the cliché used-car salesman, but Carter remembered his first car purchase fondly. Any pushiness on Billy's part had seemed to come from a conviction that he'd found the perfect car for his customers and couldn't, in good conscience, let them leave without it. And when Billy leaned heavily into a sales pitch, it was with genuine enthusiasm for his cars, evident by the fact that he called them his babies and had named most of them.

Which was why Carter was here. He could have snapped his fingers and had a car delivered from just about anywhere in the world, whenever he wanted. But coming to Billy's had seemed right—almost as though Carter had a long-dormant loyalty to Haven that had come alive the second he'd crossed the town's borders.

"Was sorry to hear about this." Billy made a sympathetic noise as he gestured at Carter's injured arm. "Got yourself a broken wing, huh? Any word on whether or not you'll get that golden arm back, or is it dunzo? I guess we all have to get old sometime."

Ooph. Carter knew the other man didn't mean it as a jab, but it felt like one all the same. The reminder that he was aging—and replaceable—seemed to hit Carter right in the solar plexus.

"Say, Billy, I saw the cutest red truck out front," Olive interjected, coming toward the two of them and gesturing toward the parking lot. "*Puh-lease* tell me it hasn't been spoken for."

"Oh, you're talking about Jody!" Billy said, turning back toward Olive, a smile beaming over his face. "That little cutie's a real doll. Been waiting for just the right home for her. Come on out, let me show you what she can do . . ."

Carter opened his mouth to remind Olive that they were here for *his* car needs, not hers, but he shut it, because though Olive didn't so much as glance his way, he somehow suspected she'd deliberately—and smoothly—directed Billy's attention away from Carter's injury.

Olive followed Billy outside into the sweltering heat, nodding enthusiastically as he rattled off horsepower and gas-mileage stats.

Carter started to follow, but a *more spry than she looked* Mona quickly stepped in front of him, her brown eyes brimming with good-natured curiosity.

She touched his arm, and he looked down at her.

"Okay, I confess I'm not the sports fan Billy is," Mona said, lowering her voice, though her husband was already outside. "But I love *Us Weekly*, and I never miss a *Citizen* magazine update! So, I have to ask . . . Is it true you dated Eden Liu, or was that tabloid gossip?"

Carter barely withheld the flinch at the mention of *Citizen* magazine—he still hadn't quite come to grips with the fact that his face would be plastered all over newsstands as Man of the Year in a few short weeks, and the story of his injury, which had finally faded out of the mainstream media, would be broadcast all over again.

"A little bit true," he said with a smile. "We went on a few dates, and she's great, but between our schedules, we figured the best we'd ever do was see each other every couple months, and parted ways as friends."

"Oh, of course, she travels all over the world for her fashion shows!" Mona said with a reverence that told him she was far more awestruck by the supermodel ex-girlfriend's accomplishments than his own, and that suited him just fine.

"What about Cameron Diaz? Have you met her?"

"Once or twice," he said noncommittally.

"I just love her," Mona said with a happy sigh. "I was disappointed at first when she retired from acting, but I've read her books!"

"Oh yeah?" Carter said, unable to keep from shifting slightly to see where Billy and Olive circled a red truck in the parking lot, Billy's arms waving wildly, and Olive nodding with equal enthusiasm.

"So now, are you seeing anyone special?" Mona asked, rather unabashedly.

He reluctantly turned his attention back to her. "Not at the current moment, no."

"Not at the current moment." She pounced, though in a friendly, puppy-dog kind of way. "Does that mean you've got your eye on a girl?"

Felicity's face flashed before his eyes. Or at least, Felicity's face as it had looked ten years ago, when they'd eagerly held each other's hands and made that stupid, stupid pact . . .

Or maybe not so stupid.

Their relationship was old news, sure, but to date, it was still his best relationship. It had been . . . sweet. Unmarred by the paparazzi, the struggles of long distance, or the vague sense that they were locked in a competition to be the most famous, as had been the case with some of his celebrity girlfriends in the past.

Who was to say they couldn't pick up where they'd left off? He was single. She was single. They were both twenty-eight, and they had said that if they were both single in ten years . . .

"Nah," he told Mona with what he hoped was a disarming smile. "Nobody on the horizon."

If he hadn't even told his own mother or twin about his and Felicity's "arrangement," he wasn't going to start with a woman who, while very sweet, seemed like the type to have her own celebrity gossip blog. Or, at the very least, to be at the top of Haven's gossip phone tree.

Instead of badgering him further, she nodded in understanding, and patted the side of his nonbroken arm gently. "Well, don't you worry. I'm sure you'll find the absolute right girl when you're not looking. But first things first, let's see about getting you a car, shall we? I know Olive's not looking for one. She just got her little used VW a year ago, and it's just right for her."

Interesting. So he'd been right, then, about Olive using her interest in the red truck to save Carter from Billy's uncomfortable questions, rather than out of actual interest in it. He felt a rush of gratitude. It had been a long time since someone had extended such a simple kindness. Sure, Carter had people jumping through hoops to support him left and right, but that was to support the *ballplayer.* Any number of people would do whatever needed to be done to keep him on the team, to heal him—anything to get him back on the field.

Far fewer cared about his happiness off the field.

Billy and Olive came back into the lobby, chatting excitedly, and Billy gave Carter an enthusiastic thump on the back. "All right, son, all right. Let's get that paperwork underway, huh? Hope your left hand's not your signing hand!"

He chuckled as he headed into the back office, and the smile of gratitude that Carter had been about to flash Olive faded. "Um, what's he talking about?"

Olive thumped him on the back, mimicking Billy's action, the gesture nearly as forceful as the man's had been. "Congrats, Baseball. You've got yourself a brand-new truck!"

"Wait. What?"

"The red one!" she said with a grin, gesturing to the parking lot.

"But I don't want a truck. Definitely not a red one."

She waved her hand. "You only say that because you haven't seen it yet."

"Sort of my point. Shouldn't I be the one to see and inspect and choose my car?"

"Shh," she said, laying her forefinger along her lips and tapping repeatedly, the way a mother might to a toddler in church. She pointed. "Billy's here with your paperwork."

Carter ground his teeth. "But I don't want—"

Three expectant faces blinked up at him, and Carter dragged his hand over his face. Ah, what the hell. He had the money. And the car was only for a few weeks.

"You got a pen?" he asked, sighing only slightly in resignation.

Mona already had one ready, and Olive was pulling out a desk chair across from Billy, gesturing for Carter to sit.

He did, but he gave Olive a pointed *we'll talk about this later* glare as he did so.

She grinned, then plopped into the chair beside him. "It's a good thing you got a truck, because you're going to want a grill while you're here, and it wouldn't have fit in a car."

He gave her a distracted look. "A grill?"

"The rental house doesn't have one. I checked. And lucky for you, Walmart has an amazing deal right now. We can drive over there next, take your new little cutie for a spin, then you can drop me back off here on the way home. That's okay, right, Billy? If we leave Bingo parked here for a few?"

"Fine by me!"

"Who the hell is Bingo?" Carter asked, even as he scanned the pages of legalese in front of him.

"My car," Olive said, as though this were obvious. "Billy named him, of course, but I kept the name, because, well, that's his name."

"Where am I?" Carter muttered. It was more under his breath than to anyone in the room, but all three answered anyway.

"You're home!" they said in cheerful unison.

So he was. So he was.

Chapter Five

Despite the fact that Haven's trendiest restaurant had been open for years, Carter had never set foot inside the highly acclaimed Cedar & Salt before tonight.

It had opened after he'd left town, and as everyone seemed hell-bent on reminding him, he didn't come back often. When he did, it was typically for holidays, and his mother made it a point to cook his favorites for every meal. Carter wasn't one to turn down macaroni and cheese topped with bread crumbs and bacon, even if it wasn't exactly the "gym fuel" his mother tried to pass it off as.

He had added an extra mile to his stationary bike ride at the gym this morning and still wasn't sure he'd burned off the extra portion of beef stroganoff his mother had heaped onto his plate when he'd gone by his parents' last night. He'd thought he'd miss running, and he did, but he didn't hate the stationary bike as much as he'd thought he would—was even looking into getting one installed in the rental home as a way to stay in shape while he was here in Haven.

But his mother had book club tonight, his dad had poker night, and poor Caitlyn had been put on bed rest for the remainder of her pregnancy. Carter had been assured it was just a precaution, but he'd stopped by his twin's house on his way to dinner, armed with Walmart's entire selection of romance novels, double-stuffed Oreos, and what he thought was a remarkable tolerance for hearing about his sister's "incompetent uterus."

He'd finally left her to her husband's impressively patient care, and followed Caitlyn's bossy insistence that Cedar & Salt was the only acceptable option for dinner.

Despite never having been to the restaurant, Carter felt immediately at home walking through the front door. It was cozy without having that *tables on top of each other* feeling of Manhattan restaurants and bustling without being loud, and its smells rivaled anything coming out of his mother's kitchen, which he would tell her *never*.

Carter gave the starstruck hostess a quick smile, well aware that the din of the restaurant had lowered to a hum when he'd walked in and been recognized, only to return to its previous volume and then some as word got around that he was in fact *the* Carter Ramsey.

Carter didn't mind. He'd gotten plenty used to it over the years as his popularity increased, though he was struck immediately by how different the feel was here in Haven. Instead of hushed, revered whispers as he passed, people made eye contact and greeted him by name—first name—as he walked by their tables on his way to the bar. The greetings were universally friendly and familiar, from both faces he recognized and ones he didn't.

Carter shook hands, exchanged hugs with his parents' friends, clamped shoulders of old classmates, and patiently listened to his piano teacher lecture him on his wasted musical talent. He enjoyed it all, but was also more than ready for a drink by the time he reached the welcoming wooden bar at the center of the restaurant.

He snagged one of the few remaining stools, then blinked in surprise when a fresh beer was pushed in front of him by the neighboring patron.

"Thought you could use this. Did I just hear Antoinette Bowens try to marry you off to her daughter?"

"You did indeed," Carter said with a laugh as he turned toward the familiar voice.

Jacob "Jakey" Kutcher had played third base to Carter's shortstop on the varsity baseball team. He'd been talented, but baseball had been more hobby than passion, and he'd stayed in Haven to work at his parents' construction business rather than pursue athletics.

Jakey's waistline had expanded slightly since high school, but his wide grin and shaggy red hair were the same.

"Hey, man," Carter said, hugging his old friend with a hearty thump on the back. "How the hell are you? How's Becky? The baby?"

Jakey was one of the few high school friends Carter tried to keep up with. Mostly just a text here and there, but enough for Carter to know the basics of his life.

"Becky's got a much-coveted invitation to your mom's book club tonight, and Grandma demanded Hannah's company, which means I have the rare free night to hear how the hell you're doing," Jakey said with an easy smile.

"Hey, Carter, you eating?" the pretty bartender said with a flirtatious smile, leaning over to showcase her impressive cleavage.

"Ah—" Carter floundered. The woman's inviting smile and vaguely seductive tone were familiar territory, but he was pretty sure he'd never met her before.

"Damn, there I go, turning invisible again!" Jakey joked. "*Two* menus. Thanks, Erika."

The bartender gave Jakey a good-natured eye roll, but she got the hint, straightening and handing over a couple of menus, then winked at Carter before sauntering over to the other side of the bar.

"Do we know her?" Carter asked under his breath.

"I do, you don't. Name's Erika. Mark Blakely hired her from out of town when he opened this place, and she's been his right-hand woman ever since. She and Mark were actually a thing for a while, even though he was hung up on Kelly Byrne. Remember them?"

"Sure," Carter replied. "Couple years ahead of us? He was quiet, she was not, but they were inseparable. Never saw one without the other."

"Inseparable and platonic, until a couple years ago," Jakey said, waggling his eyebrows.

"Yeah?" Carter asked, taking a sip of beer and enjoying the unique sense of comfort that came from good-natured small-town gossip, where most everyone had everyone else's best interests at heart.

Jakey nodded. "Yup. Married, happy, and just about everyone's favorite couple. For now."

"For now?" Carter echoed warily, catching the verbal wink in his friend's tone.

"You broke your arm, not your brain, so the playing-dumb routine's not flying," Jakey said with a friendly smile. "Any chance you'll fill old Jakey in on what everyone is wondering?"

Carter changed his mind about small-town gossip. Nothing comforting about it. It was *annoying*. He stayed silent, but his friend charged ahead anyway.

"Rumor's going around that Felicity's coming back 'to visit her cousin.'" Jakey's air quotes let Carter know what he thought of Felicity's supposed motivations.

Carter still didn't respond, and once again, Jakey pressed on.

"Come on. You both steer clear of Haven for ten years, and you just happen to roll into town right around the same time?"

"Hi, have you *met* my sister? Do you think there's any chance she'd have let me escape the high school reunion next month once she learned I was on the IL?"

"What about Felicity? She going to the reunion?"

"Beats me." Carter took another drink of his beer.

"You haven't talked to her recently?"

"Depends. Is summer after graduation recent?"

"Damn." Jakey sounded disappointed at first, then perked up. "But you could call her."

"Don't have her phone number." It was a straightforward—and truthful—response, but the reasons for that response were a little more complicated. He could have gotten her number if he'd wanted to, and yet he hadn't.

There were some things best discussed in person.

Eager for a change of subject, Carter pointed the menu up to the TV in the corner of the bar, where the nightly news showed two talking heads. "What do you think the chances are they'll change that to the game?"

"One hundred percent, but we've got a few minutes before the first pitch," his friend said, checking the time on his phone. He looked back at Carter. "Okay, so if you're not seeing Felicity, anyone else on your radar?"

"How is it that I haven't seen you in years, yet in the two minutes I've been here, we've only talked about women?"

"Cool, cool. Dodging the question," Jakey said, holding up his hands. "I get it. Prom king and queen broke up, ditched Haven the same week, have hardly come back—you barely, her not at all—until now. If I didn't try to get some details, Becky would've made me sleep on the couch tonight. She keeps telling me you guys are like a Taylor Swift song."

Carter sighed. "Sorry, man. I don't have any details. You probably know more than I do about what Felicity's been up to."

"College in California, married a Hollywood director, or producer, or something, who's like fifteen years older than her, right after graduation. She's been in LA ever since, got divorced a few months back."

"Okay, that's about exactly as much as I know," Carter admitted.

"For real?" Jakey asked, still skeptical. "You guys were like a TV couple. How have you not talked for ten years? At the very least you could have had one of your minions keep tabs on her."

"Yes, because that's what the MLB is all about. Tracking their players' high school girlfriends. And a TV couple? I thought we were a Taylor Swift song."

"You know what I mean. You were the *It* Couple, and then you were both gone."

"She was headed to California, me to the pros. Didn't work out, as high school relationships usually don't," Carter said, keeping his tone light, but also trying to insert a case-closed finality into the statement.

"Fine. At least tell me if the rumors about you and that supermodel being engaged were true. Becky will kill me if I don't bring something home."

"Which supermodel?" There had been a few.

"You know." Jakey made an elongated motion. "The one with the legs."

"They've all got legs."

"Exactly how many supermodels have you slept with that you don't know which one I'm talking about?" Jakey asked.

Carter shrugged, and Jakey whistled. "Damn. Impressive. But man, shouldn't you at least know if you were engaged to one of them?"

"Definitely never engaged. Or close to it," Carter clarified quickly. He was no monk, but neither had he had a relationship in recent memory that had lasted more than a few months. Not because he was a player who liked to bounce from one woman to the next, but because having a relationship in the spotlight was hard. Having a long-distance relationship in the spotlight was harder. He'd never met someone who seemed to care about him enough to make it through the hard parts. Had never met someone he cared about enough to fight for. Even Felicity . . .

"All right, all right, all right," Jakey said. "But what about—"

"My God," Carter said with a laugh, more amused than annoyed. "You're almost as bad as Olive."

Jakey blinked. "Olive. Olive Dunn? What's she got to do with anything?"

"I had the ill fortune of renting the house next door to hers. I've never met someone quite so . . ."

He didn't finish the sentence. *Couldn't*, because there were really no words to describe his old lab partner.

"That's Olive for you. A handful, but the good kind of handful." Jakey winced. "That came out sexual. If Becky's behind me, just shoot me now and end my misery."

Carter smiled and gave a quick glance over his friend's shoulder. "Nope, all clear—"

He broke off, because standing behind him was a woman, but not Jakey's wife.

Jakey noted Carter's expression and glanced over his shoulder as well, his face breaking out in a wide grin. "Speak of the devil. Hey, Liv." Jakey pecked Olive's cheek, not having to lean down to do so because of her taller-than-average height.

"Hello, boys." She draped an arm over Jakey's shoulder, then helped herself to some of his beer. "What's this about me being a handful?"

"A good handful," Jakey said, flashing her a grin. "Did you hear that part?"

"I did." She ruffled his hair before turning to Carter. "What about you, Baseball? Do you think I'm a good handful?"

Carter was startled to realize that it took some serious willpower not to lower his gaze to her breasts right then. He resisted, barely, but he had a good memory from the day before, and could recall that grown-up Olive Dunn in her tight jeans and plain white T-shirt would make a very nice handful indeed.

The moment passed in an instant as Olive tapped the twentysomething man to Carter's right on the shoulder and gave him a friendly smile. "Hey, Paul. Scooch on down a seat, would you?"

To Carter's bemusement, the guy gave Olive a happy, slightly adoring smile, and moved his whisky, burger, and butt down a seat, simply because she'd asked. "Happy to, Olive."

Carter noticed that Paul was less successful than he'd been in avoiding looking at her breasts.

She plopped onto the stool on Carter's other side and waved her hand to get the bartender's attention. "Hey, Erika. Can I get whatever beer these boys are drinking, and some chicken nachos? Oh, and since I'll be splitting the bill with Mr. Multimillions here, let's add extra guac. And not"—Olive held up her finger for emphasis—"that tiny little cup the size of a melon ball they try to charge me three bucks for. Tell Joel I want *proper* extra guac!"

"Yes, sir!" Erika said, pairing a patient eye roll with a smile that made Carter think she was well used to Olive's way of handling things.

"Hey look, your team!" Olive said, pointing at the TV as she reached out and stole a sip of Carter's beer, same as she had with Jakey's. "Do you want me to tell them to turn it off? I can make them, you know."

He believed her. He also noted that it was the second time in two days that Olive Dunn—a woman he barely knew—had tried to protect him.

"Nah," he said as easily as he could. "It's fine."

Olive reached out to pat his cast gently. "Are you sure? I could blindfold you. I think I have a bandanna out in Bingo. Actually, I know I do. A couple of them!"

"Why do you—never mind," he finished, since getting inside Olive's head was not something he had the energy for, now or ever. "I'll pass on the blindfold."

"Fine. Then Jakey and I will talk at you to distract you."

Jakey seemed all too happy to comply with Olive's plan, and as the two chatted more at him than with him, Carter was a little surprised to realize that watching baseball with friends in his hometown was sort of nice. Even if he wasn't playing.

Chapter Six

"Cait, if you apologize one more time, you're going to have to be on bed rest for a whole other reason," Olive said, miming bashing her friend's knees while making a popping noise, then moving to adjust the pillows behind her pregnant friend's back.

The onetime student council president, volunteer for just about everything, and career meddler in all things Haven had acquiesced to her bed rest orders just about as well as Olive herself would have: not well. Not well at all.

Despite the fact that they hadn't been close in high school, Olive had come to think of Caitlyn and her friend Kelly Blakely as her soul sisters. They were all loyal, straight-talking, and not the least bit hesitant about interfering in matters that needed interfering.

"I know, I'm sorr—*not* sorry," Caitlyn corrected herself, when Olive gave her a warning look. "It's just that I really hate leaving you to do all the planning on your own. I tried to explain to the dimwit doctor that as cochair of the reunion I couldn't be on bed rest, but she was a real pain in the—"

"Nope," Olive interrupted. "We're listening to the doc on this one. When the cervix talks, we ladies must listen. 'Tis biology's idea of hilarity. Hey, did you know my uterus is just a little bit—wonky? Twisted?

Shoot, what was the word that Dr. Khalid used? Janky? No, that doesn't seem right . . ."

"*Annnnnndd* that's my cue to drop these off and make a very fast getaway, preferably toward some experimental memory procedure that will let me forget I've heard any of this," Carter said from the doorway, looking like he wanted to make good on his threat to flee the room. Or the continent.

"Hey! My famous brother is here. What did you bring me today?" Caitlyn said, making grabby hands toward the bag he held in his right arm.

Olive already knew what he'd brought her. It was the same generic bag that Josefin's Patisserie used when their flighty salesclerk forgot to order more of their usual pink-branded bags, with their logo printed on the side.

Caitlyn opened the bag, pulled out a pink box, and proved Olive right. "Macarons!"

Carter shrugged. "I remember when Aunt Joyce and Uncle Vick went to Paris over Christmas and brought you back a box. You liked those gross cookies even better than you liked the Chanel wallet you insisted you 'wanted more than anything.'"

"True, true. I was going through a Francophile phase," she said to Olive. "I wore a beret and everything. It was terrible."

"It was," Carter agreed. "She also took up cigarettes as part of her cause and got grounded for life."

"It was two cigarettes. More like one and a half, because they were so nasty. Even still, yes, I was grounded for life. But hey! At least the French cookies are still good," Caitlyn said, extending the box to Olive. "Try one."

They are not good, Carter mouthed to Olive.

Olive looked down at the rainbow-colored cookies that, while admittedly very pretty, did not call out to her the way a hearty brownie would. "I usually stick with the éclairs when I go into Josefin's. And actually, I more often find myself going for the M&M cookies at Willa's. Or basically, anything chocolate."

"There," Caitlyn said, pointing to a brown one. "Chocolate. Eat, and be changed."

Olive fished it out of the box and bit into half.

"Well?" Caitlyn demanded.

Olive swallowed. "I'm torn between being scared of your pregnancy hormones and admitting that this is just sort of . . . okay."

Caitlyn gasped, grabbed the remaining half of the cookie out of Olive's hand, and stuffed it in her own mouth. "I cannot believe that you're taking his side. But you guys ganging up on me does rather nicely set up the reason why I summoned you here today."

"Oh, is that what you call this text? A summoning?" Carter asked, pulling his cell out of his back pocket. "Because if you read the actual words, it sounds more like a death threat."

"And Mom said I was the dramatic one growing up," Caitlyn retorted, biting into a pink cookie. "I guess I just got it out of my system earlier, and now it's your turn. Anyway. I've brought you both to my makeshift infirmary slash bed prison to discuss a mutual need."

"Oh God," Carter said.

Olive had to admit, she shared his apprehension. She was all about solving problems—she just liked to be the one *creating* the solution, not being assigned to it.

"You," Caitlyn said, pointing at her twin, "have nothing to do but pine for your missing ex-girlfriend and let your cracked bone heal for the next several weeks. And you"—she pivoted her pointer finger to Olive—"have an entire high school reunion to plan, and your extremely capable partner has just been laid up by an unborn angel." Caitlyn rested her hand on her stomach.

"If it's coming out of you, I'd say we're fifty-fifty on angel or the other thing," Carter said.

"Hush. The point is, I can't do much to help Olive other than the stupid crap like stuffing envelopes, which leaves her without a cochair."

"If you're suggesting what I think you're suggesting, I will take those cookies away," Carter said.

"And I will make good on my kneecapping threat," Olive added.

"Damn." Carter gave Olive an appraising look. "That's dark."

Olive shrugged.

"I'm being practical!" Caitlyn protested. "Olive needs a cochair. Carter needs an activity."

Carter scowled. "I'm not a restless five-year-old boy on a rainy day."

"Well, then stop sulking like one and be agreeable," Caitlyn said. "Olive needs help."

"Actually, I really don't. I'm used to doing things by myself," Olive said, truthfully. She liked Carter way more than she would have expected to, and he was certainly easy on the eyes, but she was fairly sure he'd only get in her way. "In fact, I like doing things by myself, and I'm good at it."

"Uh-huh." Caitlyn folded her hands atop her massive belly. "And how did those posters to put up around town turn out? The ones with the glitter that we found on YouTube?"

Carter's head snapped up. "*Green* glitter?"

Olive held up a hand and gave him a warning glance. "Not a word. Not one single word."

"So *that's* what that was about," he said with a slow smile. "Our school colors are green and black."

"Oh really, are they?" she snapped. "As the lone chair of this year's Haven High reunion, I wasn't aware of our school colors."

Her snippy tone only made his eyes light more gleefully, and she immediately took back her thoughts about him being tolerable. The man was insufferable.

"Come on, Olive," Caitlyn said, nudging her friend's arm with a pale blue cookie before eating it. "We don't have the food figured out.

We haven't found anyone to sponsor the open bar, or any bar. We don't know the decor; we don't even know the theme—"

"What?" Carter made an exaggerated gasp, laying his palm over his chest. "No theme, you say? Should the show even go on?"

Carter's grin widened in direct inverse of Olive's eyes, which narrowed to slits at his insulting sarcasm.

"You're so right," Olive said to Carter in a perfectly pleasant tone. "All the things we undertake here in Haven are so silly and simple. Nothing like playing the exact same game nearly every single day for . . . a decade? That must be an absolute brain buster!" She used her hand to mime an exploding motion near her temple, complete with sound effects. *Mind blown.*

This time, it was Carter's eyes that narrowed. "Played a lot of baseball, have ya?"

Olive shrugged. *How hard can it be?*

Carter smiled, and this time it was slow and lethal. "How about a deal, Olive? I'll be your minion on all things high school reunion, if you learn how to play baseball. Let's say five sessions. At the end, we'll have a frank discussion over who has it easier."

"Oh, you do have Haven High's softball game against Rhinebeck in a couple weeks!" Caitlyn chimed in. "We always lose."

Olive gave her friend a death look, and the usually indomitable Caitlyn flinched and mouthed, *Sorry.*

Carter lifted a single eyebrow in challenge, a solid villain move that Olive had always respected and never been able to master.

"All right, you've got a deal." She rounded the foot of Caitlyn's bed to shake on it.

Olive never issued or accepted a challenge she wasn't confident she could crush. But when Carter's large hand closed over hers, she had an uncomfortable, irrational flicker of foreboding that in this game, there would be no winners.

Chapter Seven

While most of her friends in college had been obsessing about the freshman fifteen and frantically wiping dressing off the bits of kale in their salads, Olive had taken a different course of action and decided that since she was never going to be tiny, she might as well be strong.

She'd even enlisted the help of the quarterback of her university's football team to teach her the weight machines in the fitness center. Randal Wade had later told her he'd been so startled by the bold request that he'd said yes without thinking.

It had worked out better than either had imagined. They'd become fast, if unlikely, friends, and kept in touch over the years, even after he'd gone pro. She'd been at his wedding, and his wife's engagement shower.

And Olive still put Randal's workout lessons from all those years ago to good use. She went to the gym at least four times a week and, even on her off days, made a point to lunge her way from the sofa to the fridge rather than simply walk.

On the days she did go to the gym, she dragged herself to the elliptical on a regular basis, in the name of heart health, but for her, the weights were where it was at. Olive loved the burn, loved the gains, the power. In addition to choosing strong over small in college, in recent years she'd decided to embrace defined quads over a thigh gap.

An early riser by necessity, if not by nature (such was the life of a schoolteacher who liked to work out in the morning), Olive typically had the gym mostly to herself in the hours after it first opened. She took advantage of the solitude to take a photo of said quads to send to Randal, which would be inappropriate except she included his wife, too, though Olive was pretty sure Serena knew regardless that she wasn't a threat.

Especially considering she hadn't shaved her legs in—she looked closer at the photo—a while. The peach fuzz was definitely visible in the photo. Oh well. She hit "Send."

"Sexting so early in the morning?"

Olive jumped, surprised at the unexpected interruption. And unwanted company.

She wrinkled her nose and gave Carter an irritated once-over. "What are you doing here?"

Since the sleek black sweatpants, black performance tee, and red training shoes made it pretty obvious, instead of answering, he came toward where she sat on the bench and pulled her cell phone out of her hands.

"Hey!" She tried to snatch it back, but he'd already pulled the phone out of reach and was staring at the screen in disbelief.

"You're sexting Randal Wade? *The* Randal Wade?"

"I'm not sexting anyone," she said, standing, then snatching her phone back and locking it.

"But that's a different Randal, right? Not the starting quarterback for the Bears?"

"Wouldn't you like to know," she said with a smug smile.

"Holy shit, it *is* that Randal," he said in disbelief. "How the hell did you pull that off? Did you interfere in his life, too?"

"Yeah, because that's what I do. Stalk pro athletes."

He nodded. "That's good to hear. Very good to hear. Acceptance and acknowledging the problem is a very strong first step, Olive."

She made a shooing nose. "Go away. I've got reps to do."

He grinned. "Oh, I know."

She narrowed her eyes in suspicion. "What is that? What is that tone? I don't like it."

Carter put a foot on the bench and leaned toward her. "Our deal, remember? I help you with the reunion, you see what it's like to be a pro ball player."

"Yes, well, I'd be delighted to play catch with you later, but right now I have work to do," she said.

"We'll 'play catch' at some point, but you owe me five practice rounds, and the first starts right now."

Olive wrinkled her nose and looked at him skeptically.

"You know what percentage of my time is spent with a ball or bat in my hand?" he asked.

Delighting in the double entendre, Olive lifted her eyebrows and gave him a slow smile. "Color me *very* interested in those statistics." She playfully reached out and dragged a finger along his shin, smiling wider when he knocked her hand away.

"Less than twenty percent," he continued. "I spend more time in the gym than I do on the field, more time training than I do playing the game. So you'd better prepare your fine ass to see how it's done."

She perked up. "You think my ass is fine?"

"I think it will be once I get done with it."

Olive batted her eyelashes and fanned her face. "Why, Mr. Ramsey. You presume too much."

"I meant after you do some squats—you know what, never mind. We'll start with arms. I'll spot you."

"No, thanks." She went to breeze past him.

He shifted, blocking her path. "Unless you'd like to cancel our deal?"

"I'm not canceling anything. I just thought we could keep the whole baseball thing between us."

"Afraid someone will see you at something you're not good at?"

Olive gritted her teeth, hating that he'd hit the nail on the head. She prided herself in being competent at all things, if not the best in all things.

So, yes, she did tend to avoid things she didn't excel at, which included baseball or anything requiring hand-eye coordination. She didn't particularly like when people noticed that fact, and most didn't. The fact that he, a pretty boy who didn't even live here anymore, had picked up on it after being around her for less than a week was disturbing.

But this wasn't baseball. Or even a stupid work-sponsored softball game. She could do the gym, and do it well. And if he wanted to count a good old-fashioned workout as the first of their *learn what it's like to be me* game, then she'd count herself lucky.

"You're not going to go easy on me, are you?" she asked skeptically.

"Why don't we find out?"

There was an unfamiliar honeyed note to his tone that she didn't like. Didn't like at all.

She wrinkled her nose. "Cryptic and flirty may get you all the Manhattan girls, but up here in Haven, we women like it straight up."

His eyebrows lifted, and she realized it was she who'd made the sexual innuendo, and rather than backing away from it, she lifted her eyebrows in challenge back at him.

Carter laughed and shook his head, apparently conceding the point to her, because he changed the subject. "You never said how you know Randal Wade." He came toward her, watching as she picked up a weight and moved it to the bar for her bench press.

"We're friends."

"Huh," Carter said thoughtfully. "Were you ever more than friends?"

"Have you ever met Randal?" she countered.

"We've attended the same charity things once or twice."

"Okay, so picture him," Olive said. "Now look at me."

She glanced up to see if he'd done as she'd instructed, and was disconcerted to find that he was indeed looking at her, and looking rather . . . thoroughly. His gaze traveled from the tips of her neon-green cross-trainers, up over her bare legs and short shorts, and to the cropped tank that was neon green as well, though not quite the same shade as her shoes, and thus clashed terribly.

"You see?" she said, striving for nonchalance, even though she felt strangely tingly. Olive wasn't unfamiliar with sexual attraction, but it had been a while since she'd experienced it firsthand. One of the consequences of living in a small town where you'd known everyone . . . forever. She'd known Carter forever, too, but at the moment it was really hard to look at him and recall the kid she'd gone to kindergarten with. All she could see was man.

"I see that you do this a lot," he replied, blissfully unaware of her train of thought.

"Do what, try to get rid of people who interrupt my gym time? Correct." She settled onto the bench.

"Work out," he replied. "You're strong."

Strong. Not beautiful, not hot. *Strong*. She'd take it.

"Damn straight, I'm strong," she said. "But news flash, strong is not what Randal Wade types seek in a mate."

"Maybe it's because you use the word *mate*."

"I'm a biology teacher. What do you expect?"

He blinked. "You are? How did I miss that?"

She smiled. "You never asked. Why did you think I had the summer off?"

"Huh. I guess I hadn't thought about it. Funny, though, that we were lab partners, and you turned out to be a science teacher."

"Yes, hilarious. Now, much as I'd love to sit here and reminisce about our first-rate Haven education, are we going to actually work out, or what?"

He gestured to the bench. "I'll spot you."

"I don't need a spotter."

"For bench press? I think you do."

"I'm not going for a PR. I know how many reps I can do safely with this weight."

"This is my gig, remember? And the way I do this, safety comes first. How much do you usually lift?"

She told him, and he finished placing the weights before moving into a spotting position and lifting his eyebrows. *I'm waiting.*

Olive started to lift the bar, and his free hand immediately came nearer, ready to assist when needed.

She frowned. "Hold up. You can't be my spotter. You're down an arm."

Carter smiled. "Sit up."

He nodded with his chin for her to move, and curious, she did.

His long fingers wrapped around the bar, and the muscles of his uninjured arm flexed as he lifted the bar from the rack, lowering and lifting it with relative ease. He repeated the process, and with the third rep, she snapped at him.

"Okay, okay, I get it, you're super strong. Quit hijacking my workout."

He set the bar back, and she returned to her earlier position, doing her best to ignore him altogether as she finally got around to starting her set.

Only . . . it was harder than she expected to ignore your spotter. Almost impossible to ignore a spotter like Carter Ramsey.

The positioning alone was, um, *intimate*, with his crotch disturbingly near her head, his eyes watching her every motion, his hand hovering in the general vicinity of her chest.

The fact that it was him was so much worse. Tall, muscular, and she had to admit, this was a very good angle to observe all of his best features . . .

"Quit ogling me," Carter said, never taking his gaze away from the rise and fall of the bar.

"Take it easy, Captain America. You're the one who insisted on straddling my face."

"Captain America?"

"You're not hot enough to be Thor," she said, pushing through the last rep of her set and replacing the bar. Normally she'd have pushed herself a bit further, but she didn't usually have Carter Ramsey watching her every move.

He may not be Thor, but his presence was increasingly distracting. But also kind of . . . motivating. Before she knew it, she had finished her reps and did a double take when she saw what she'd just lifted. It was a PR after all.

But Carter had no intention of letting her gloat. He moved to the rack of free weights. "How about some incline dumbbell curls?" he asked, picking up a dumbbell that was just out of her comfort zone, but doable.

Olive groaned. She hated curls—boring—but she did them, as well as every other exercise he threw at her over the next hour, her only breaks coming when he squeezed in a couple of exercises of his own, which together they figured out how to modify, given his out-of-commission left arm.

"What's the tattoo?" she asked, noticing the same ink she'd seen the first day peeking out beneath the sleeve of his shirt—just enough to be visible, not enough for her to know what she was looking at.

Olive reached to flick a playful finger over the exposed skin, the gesture instinctive and friendly, though the second her finger touched his arm, she realized her mistake—the move was too intimate. His gaze snapped to hers, just as she snatched her hand back.

What was that?!

"You do this every day?" she asked hurriedly, striving to push past the moment. "This routine?"

"For my morning workout, it's pretty standard."

Her eyes bugged. "Your *morning* workout? You have more than one?"

"Every day," he said, his tone holding no trace of gloat or taunt, just simple fact.

"Damn," she muttered, squirting some water in her mouth. "Well, I've got to hand it to you. It was challenging but also sort of . . . fun."

He smiled, looking genuinely pleased with her praise. "I'm glad. Now, how about a quick five-mile sesh on the stationary bikes before we do our hour of stretching?"

Olive started to laugh. Until she realized he wasn't joking.

Chapter Eight

"Now, you know I'm not one to guilt, but my friends have taken note that my baby boy's been back home for nearly a week, and just now are *both* of my babies coming over at the same time so we can have a family dinner."

"But she's not one to guilt," Caitlyn said to Carter under her breath as she pulled the plate of her mother's stuffed mushrooms closer to her. "And since when does *four days* round up to an entire week?"

"She brings up a solid point," Carter agreed, reaching out for a mushroom and popping it into his mouth as he leaned back in the same kitchen chair that he'd once done his math homework in. "Also, what are the chances we can nix the Baby Boy stuff?" he asked with a grin toward his mother.

"But you *are* my baby boy," she said, cupping his cheeks and giving him a fond look before patting just a little harder than necessary. "Who neglects me horribly."

"Why is this guilt trip reserved for me?" he said, pointing to his sister, who was getting off easy.

"Because she sees me all the time," Caitlyn said. "And I've been on bed rest, so I get a pass on account of Unborn."

"Speaking of, are you sure you should be out and about?"

"By out and about, you mean plopped in this chair with my feet up?" Caitlyn said. "Don't worry, I've done very little moving. One of the perks of being married to a firefighter is that even six months pregnant, he can carry me just about anywhere I want to go. The other perk is—"

"No," Carter interrupted. "Just no. Where is AJ? Did he finally spot your horns and go running for the hills?"

"Mom sent him to the store."

"*You* sent him to the store," Tracy Ramsey corrected. "I said that the strawberry shortcake would taste just as good without whipped cream."

"Whipped cream is the only reason to eat a fruit dessert," Carter and Caitlyn said at the exact same time.

Their mother shook her head. "If you guys are going to do that Twin Thing, at least use it for something important."

"Dessert is vitally important," Caitlyn said.

Carter nodded in solemn agreement.

"Fine." Tracy threw up her hands. "I know better than to go up against both of you. Carter, Baby Boy, what have you been up to since you've been back?"

"Probably the same thing he was up to back in high school," Warren Ramsey said, half his attention on the television in the living room. "Chasing girls. Well, the one girl."

"Still is," Caitlyn said around a stuffed mushroom. "Only it's a different girl."

"Oh?" his mother asked too casually, as she topped off her glass of Chardonnay.

"I'd like to state for the record that I'm unimpressed with your acting," Carter said to his mom. "You clearly know exactly who Cait's talking about."

"I can't help it that I'm well connected," his mom said with a shrug.

"That's one word for it," Carter said teasingly. "Who's your source?"

Tracy pointed at her husband, whose attention on the TV had him completely oblivious to the conversation.

"Dad?" Carter asked incredulously. Warren was well liked in the community, but he didn't exactly have his finger on the pulse of Haven's gossip chain the way Tracy did.

"What?" Carter's dad turned back to him, then did a double take when he saw his son's expression. "What'd I do? What'd I miss?"

"How did you know that Carter's been hanging around with Olive?" Caitlyn asked, sounding both awed and impressed.

"She came into the office this afternoon and mentioned it. I guess I said something to your mother. I didn't realize we'd be having a family meeting about it, or I'd have taken notes."

"Olive's a patient?" Caitlyn asked, propping her chin on her hand and giving their father her best smile. "What for?"

Warren Ramsey gave her the usual *don't bother* expression he used whenever someone dared to suggest he violate doctor-patient confidentiality.

"Oh, come on, none of your dermatology buddies have to know," Caitlyn begged around another mushroom. "Psoriasis? Eczema? Funky mole? Not Botox, her skin's too good."

"Rash caused from skin being aggravated by, say, glitter?" Carter guessed.

His dad gave him a surprised look, which told him that he'd guessed correctly, and Carter grinned as he filed it away. He was rapidly learning it never hurt to have some ammunition in his back pocket where Olive was concerned.

"And," his mother chimed in, "Lynn's son works at the gym and saw you two working out together."

"Just think," Caitlyn said. "I had to use all my manipulative power to get Carter to hang out in Haven while he's injured by dangling Felicity, and the real carrot was here the whole time."

"I do like Olive," his father said.

"Oh my God!" Carter said, plowing his fingers into his hair, exasperated. "I am not seeing Olive Dunn."

"Well, technically you *are* seeing her. A lot," Caitlyn pointed out.

"Because we're neighbors. And because you tricked us into that ridiculous arrangement," he snapped at his sister.

"Oh?" Tracy said again.

He pointed at his mother. "Stop with that."

"Okay, but this is something I don't know," Tracy said, setting her spatula aside and joining them at the table. "What arrangement?"

"Ooh, I get to tell," Caitlyn said, doing a happy dance in her chair. "So, I asked Carter to help Olive plan our high school reunion, since I'm not much use because of the bed rest thing. They started sniping at each other, and Olive basically pointed out that all Carter does is play the same game all day every day for the past hundred years, and how hard could that be . . ."

"Ah," Tracy said in understanding, looking at Carter. "And you decided to prove to her exactly how hard it could be. That's what the workout was about?"

That's what the workout was *supposed* to be about. The plan had been to show her just how hard staying in top shape was, and he'd fully expected her to wave the white flag in five minutes.

But she'd proven him wrong. She'd been pushing herself, yes, but she also hadn't been close to calling it quits. Even more surprising, she'd seemed to enjoy the strenuous workout.

Most surprising of all, he'd enjoyed working out with her.

"Pretty much," he said noncommittally to his mother. He loved his mom. But if she thought even for a second a woman had piqued his interest, she'd start shopping for a mother-of-the-groom dress.

And if she did get that in her head about a woman, it sure as hell shouldn't be about Olive.

He took a sip of beer, wondering how to bring it up casually, then decided his family would see right through him anyway, and went for the question he really wanted to ask. "I don't suppose any of your connections knows if the rumors about Felicity are true. Is she coming back for the reunion?"

The room fell silent for a moment, and Carter understood why. Until Caitlyn had mentioned her name on the phone to get him to come to town, they hadn't talked about Felicity in years. His mom and sister had tried ten years ago to get him to talk about their breakup, and even his dad had seemed curious, but Carter had remained stubbornly silent, and eventually they'd let it drop.

"Is who coming back for the reunion?" Carter's brother-in-law asked, coming into the kitchen carrying two cans of whipped cream, because he knew the Ramsey twins well.

"Felicity George," Caitlyn said, reaching up to pat her husband's cheek. "You remember her, she and Carter dated our senior year?"

"Sure," AJ said, opening the fridge to put the whipped cream away. "Cute brunette. Soccer player. Her cousin works with me at the station and just mentioned her today—she's staying with him and his wife when she gets into town next week."

Caitlyn stared at her mom. "Wait. Have AJ and Dad both out-gossiped us today?"

"I think so," Tracy said, sounding equally awed, before turning her attention to Carter. "So are you thinking of . . . reconciling with Felicity?"

Something like that. Maybe. I don't know.

Even though she'd been his primary reason for returning, he wasn't in any big hurry to get in touch. Every time he thought about it, he felt a little . . . tired. Or maybe it was just good old-fashioned nerves.

"It'll be good to see her," Carter said, as noncommittally as possible.

"Anyone mind if I watch the game?" Warren interjected quickly, accurately sensing the sharks circling and wanting no part of it. The question was asked casually, as though out of politeness for leaving the family discussion to watch TV, but Carter felt his father's gaze on him and knew that he was really asking if Carter minded his dad watching his team play even when he wasn't on the field.

Carter smiled to reassure him. "Go for it. Holler if anything good happens."

He no longer felt as sharp a pang that he wasn't playing, but neither was he in the mood to watch the game. It hadn't been as painful as he'd thought, watching it the other night with Olive and Jakey, but that's when he'd had Olive's nonstop chatter in his ear. It was pretty hard to feel depressed in the presence of her relentless energy.

"The kid at shortstop's not bad, but he's no Carter Ramsey," AJ told Carter.

Carter nodded in thanks at the loyalty. His brother-in-law was a good guy. A few years older than Carter and Caitlyn, he'd been a senior running back on the football team to Carter's freshman shortstop on the baseball team. As a Haven firefighter these days, AJ was as fit at thirty-one as he'd been at seventeen, but as they exchanged a look, Carter wondered if AJ got it more than most people. If he understood that it didn't matter how fit you were for your age, you were still your age, and there was always another rookie waiting to steal your spotlight—or in AJ's case, a younger, brawnier firefighter whose youth you couldn't compete with.

"Go," Caitlyn said, too distracted by her pregnancy appetite and the wheel of brie on the table to notice the moment between her twin and husband. She waved AJ in the direction of the television. "But leave the boy. I have questions."

Carter pointed at himself. "Am I the boy?"

"You are four minutes older than me, but infinitely less wise. So, yes, of course you're the boy," she said.

"Caitlyn, honey, have some grapes with the crackers," Tracy said, spinning the cheeseboard around to point the fruit at her daughter. "Babies like grapes."

"Yeah? Then how come they don't like wine?" Caitlyn asked, with a wistful glance at her mother's glass of Chardonnay.

Tracy rubbed a hand over Caitlyn's baby bump. "Just a couple more months. Then I can babysit, and you and AJ can have all the wine you want, so long as you pump."

"That's my cue," Carter said, climbing to his feet. He may not be dying to see the Hawks game, but it beat hearing about his sister's boobs.

His mom's hand reached out to grab his wrist. "Sit." Her hand was small, her frame petite, but her voice more authoritative than any Navy SEAL commander.

Carter sat.

"So," his mother said with a sweet smile, "does Olive know that Felicity's coming back to town?"

"I don't know how to make this more clear," he said, a little desperately. "Olive and I are not a thing."

"Just neighbors. And workout buddies. And she helped you pick out your shiny new truck. And you had dinner at Cedar & Salt together . . . ," his mother trailed off.

He stared at her. "Do any of your sources work for the CIA?"

"I'm just saying," she said in that tone that said there was nothing *just* about it, "it's a lot of time with her, and Olive is a very attractive woman."

"Great boobs," Caitlyn agreed.

"And now we're back to boobs," he said, tapping the bottom of the kitchen table frantically. "Is there no panic button here? There should be if I'm subjected to talking about boobs with my mom and sister."

"Not even great boobs like Olive's?" Caitlyn asked, wiggling her eyebrows.

"I am not interested in Olive's boobs," Carter lied. He had the line at the ready, because he'd repeated it to himself all damn morning when said features had looked really good in her sports bra. "And if there's no panic button, do you at least have anything stronger than this beer?"

"Whiskey above the fridge," his mom said, relenting on her no-spirits-before-dinner rule, but not, apparently, on the Olive topic of conversation. "So, were you two friends in high school?"

"Lab partners. Senior-year chemistry," he replied, standing to retrieve the whiskey.

"Did you get an A? Of course you did, if Olive was your partner," Caitlyn said.

"I can't remember. Probably. She was very into science."

"She gets that from her father," Tracy said.

Carter turned around, a bottle of Woodford Reserve in hand. "Yeah?"

When Olive had mentioned being a biology teacher today, he'd realized just how little he knew about her, and he had to admit . . . he was curious.

"Sure. Dennis Dunn was a nice man."

"Was?" Carter asked, feeling an immediate surge of sympathy for Olive.

"He passed a few years ago from lung cancer. He went very quickly after his diagnosis, which I imagine was both a blessing and a curse."

"What about her mom?" Carter asked, hoping to get a little more insight into the mystery that was Olive. As much as she seemed to be an open book on the surface—and as much as he suspected she viewed herself as an open book—there was something else about her, something that drew him to her, that he couldn't identify.

"Never in the picture. I'm not sure the story there," Tracy mused. "But Dennis did as good a job as he could raising a girl on his own. He was a pharmaceutical researcher up at that facility in Rensselaer."

"That's a long commute," Caitlyn said. "I wonder why he didn't live closer to work."

"I asked him exactly that at one of your terrible spring musicals back in the day—sorry, but they really were terrible. He said it was because of Haven's school district. He wanted the best for Olive's education, even if it meant a longer drive for him."

"Aww. That is a good dad," Caitlyn said.

"And it paid off," Tracy said. "Not only did Olive help our Carter get an A in chemistry, but everyone knows she's the best teacher at Haven High these days."

"Does she also get a parade?" Carter asked jokingly, grabbing a glass for his bourbon.

"What do you mean?"

"Everywhere I turn, people are singing Olive's praises. It's like she can do no wrong."

"Well, she's a little stubborn," Caitlyn said. "Independent, too, like to a scary degree."

Their mother took a sip of her wine. "Maybe she's independent because she has to be. No family. Living on the outskirts of town."

"Which she seems to love," Carter pointed out.

"Oh, I'm sure she does," his mother agreed quickly. "I'm just saying, I wonder if sometimes Olive isn't independent so much as . . . alone."

Carter's back was to his family, but his head snapped up in surprise at that. Who would have thought? Maybe he and Olive Dunn had something in common after all.

Chapter Nine

Olive frowned in annoyance at the knock at her front door. "What! Come in! Jeez!" she shouted from the kitchen.

A moment later Carter entered, holding a bottle of wine. "Such a gentle, welcoming greeting."

"We're neighbors. You don't need to knock," she said in exasperation, as she shook a stamp off her thumb, then hissed in irritation when it landed faceup on the counter. "Now look what you made me do. I wasted a Forever stamp."

"How did I make you do that?"

"Never mind. Good call on the wine," she said, gesturing with her head toward the cabinets. "But I'll warn you right now, if you spill on the invitations, you have to pay to replace them. I'm already a little over budget."

"Spend it all on glitter?" he asked, getting two wineglasses down.

"Oh fantastic," she said sarcastically, fishing her corkscrew out of a kitchen drawer. "At least if your baseball career goes to hell, you've got a real knack for comedy."

"I'm multitalented. Though"—he looked down at the wine bottle and his sling—"opening wine bottles is not one of my skills at this particular stage of my life."

Olive was already reaching for the bottle. She looked at the label. "Zinfandel. Nice. Are you looking forward to spending an entire night in each other's company?"

"I promise I go down a bit easier with some wine," he said.

"Hubba-hubba." Olive made a joking thrusting motion with her hips as she opened the wine. "That's a bit forward."

He held out a wineglass for her to pour into, then the other. "You're a big fan of your sex jokes, huh?"

"*Go down a bit easier?* Come on. How could I not swing for the fences?"

"An oral sex reference *and* a baseball reference. Careful, or I'll fall in love with you."

Olive snorted at the comment, because she was supposed to, but it had caused an annoying little flicker deep in a part of her heart that she tried very, very hard to ignore. People didn't fall in love with Olive Dunn.

"I like your place," he said, already changing the subject.

"Well, of course," she said. "It's rather fabulous."

It was true. Olive loved her home. Mostly because it was hers, and it looked like her. She'd spent a year renovating and decorating it just right, and she liked to think of the final results as "industrial chic." She'd kept the old house's original brick walls as well as the original hardwood floors and then contrasted the classic "old" look with modern pieces— brushed stainless steel appliances, crisp white furniture, exposed-bulb lighting fixtures. And her personal favorite: a smattering of lime-green accent pieces, because it was her favorite color.

The place was feminine and personal, and Carter Ramsey, in all his maleness, looked a little out of place. For that matter, any man would look out of place in it. Something she was just now realizing, because there hadn't been a man other than her father in her house in . . . well, a while.

He looked at her in bemusement. "You're really confident. About your home. About yourself."

"Well, sure. What's not to like?" she said, patting his cheek and then turning back to the counter, where she'd spread out the stacks of invitations and envelopes. "You ready for this?"

Carter gave the mailer supplies an aggravated look. "Do we have to?"

"Part of our deal, remember? You said you wanted to know what it was like to be me."

"Uh, revisionist history," he said. "I'm positive I did not say that."

"You know what I mean. You thought planning a reunion was no big deal, so here's your shot. Run point on this."

"You're not helping?"

"Of course I'll help," she said, sipping her wine and giving him a sly smile. "Just tell me what to do."

Olive wasn't above feeling extremely satisfied when he gave the various paper piles a panicked look. *Welcome to the real world, Mr. Pro Athlete.*

He held up his wine. "Can I finish this first?"

"You may," she said with a smile, before pointing at her kitchen table. "Sit. Tell me all your secrets: third nipple, weird sex fetish where you get really turned on by shampoo, your favorite food is raw beets, and you eat them before every meal."

He shook his head, but he sat, and she went to join him, tucking a leg beneath her and hiding a smile when his eyes tracked the motion, his green gaze clearly appreciating that her short shorts left most of her leg bare.

"My secrets, huh?" he said, lifting his eyes back to hers.

"Or something interesting. You choose. We have a boring task ahead. I want to be entertained."

"Secret, or interesting fact," he mused, tapping long fingers against her wood table. "All right. I've got one that might be both."

She gestured with her hand. *Try me.*

Carter blew out a breath and stared down at his wineglass. "*Citizen* magazine named me their Man of the Year."

Olive's mouth dropped open. She wasn't surprised—or starstruck—often, but *Citizen* magazine was huge. And Man of the Year was their biggest issue.

"Seriously?" she said. "As in, the same award they gave to the freaking New York City mayor last year?"

"Well, he's not mayor anymore," Carter pointed out.

"Exactly. Because he's running for Congress," Olive said. "And everybody's already talking about how the White House is next. You're in the same category as that?"

"You don't have to sound so scandalized," he said, sounding irritated.

"Sorry, sorry," she backpedaled quickly. "It's a big honor. Right?"

"It's a weird honor," he said slowly. "Not one that I ever imagined when I envisioned my future."

"What did you imagine?" she asked curiously. Haven was a small enough town that she'd known Carter—albeit loosely—since elementary school, and as long as she could remember, it had always been a foregone conclusion that he would go places. Mainly, to the majors. He was in a different league, literally, and thus she'd never really given him much thought.

For the first time, she wondered about what that sort of youth must have been like for him.

"I never really thought much beyond the fact that I love baseball, and my hope was to be able to play it for as long as I could, or as long as they'd let me."

Olive nodded, careful not to let her gaze drop to his injured arm.

"Which," he continued with a little laugh, "is ironic now, I guess."

"Why ironic?"

"*Citizen* sent me an early copy of the issue. As part of my contract, I get right of approval on feature stories about me."

"Is it not good? Did they out your weird shampoo fetish?"

"No, it's fine. And I don't have any weird fetishes, at least none that I've discovered," he said, with a quick smile. "It's just . . ." Carter sighed. "It's all about baseball. Or rather about my baseball skill."

"Well, yeah. That's sort of your thing," Olive pointed out.

"I know, but—" He stood and paced around her kitchen. "Weirdly, it didn't occur to me until that issue, until this"—he lifted the arm in the sling as best he could—"that baseball is all I have. It's all that I am."

Olive took a sip of wine as she thought this over. "Hmm." She took another sip of wine. "Hmm," she repeated. "That is some deep stuff."

"I know," he said with a laugh, sitting down once more. "Sorry, forget it."

"No, I won't forget it," she said, placing a hand on his, and trying to ignore the unexpected flick of heat in her stomach when his gaze snapped to hers. "I imagine that must be really difficult. To put your entire life into one thing, and then realize that it won't last forever. To not know what comes next, or even what lies beneath all that skill."

Carter stared at her hard, and the slight vulnerability she saw hiding beneath his usual masculinity and charm tugged at her. Gave her the courage to continue.

"But there *is* something lying beneath," she said, pressing her hand to his. "You're more than your sweet, sweet baseball skills."

"Yeah?" He gave a quick smile. "I don't suppose you happen to know what lies beneath?"

"Not yet. But we'll figure it out," she said, giving his hand a friendly pat, then pulling back to lighten the moment. "I'll help."

He laughed. "You seem very accustomed to people doing as you say. Not to mention certain that it'll go your way."

"It's a confidence thing, sort of a must as a teacher. If the kids think even for a second that you're unclear or unsure about something, they'll wiggle right in there and turn your entire lesson plan upside down."

"My mom says you're the best teacher at Haven High."

She laughed. "I'm a good teacher, but most of the teachers are good. Our dropout rate is low, our test scores are high, and most importantly to me, kids seem to like being there."

"Do you like being there?"

She opened her mouth, then shut it, realizing that nobody had ever asked her that before. "I love being a teacher."

"Not what I asked."

No, it wasn't. Carter Ramsey was a jock, but he was no cliché jock dummy who only had a brain for baseball stats. He was quick-witted and a good deal more perceptive than she'd expected.

"All right," she said with a slightly nervous laugh. "In return for your sharing, I'll take a turn, but don't get excited, nobody's putting me on a magazine cover." She took a breath. "So, I love being a teacher, I love Haven High, but . . . I don't agree with my boss's philosophy." She said it on a rush, then realized it wasn't quite accurate. "Actually, it's not just that I don't agree with it. I don't respect it."

"Who's your boss?"

"Principal Mullins."

"What happened to Principal Glover?"

"Shockingly," Olive said with a smile, "Mary Glover dared to want to retire to spend some time with her grandkids after corralling us hooligans for the better part of three decades. Kirk took over for her a couple years ago."

"And you don't like him?"

"He's fine," she hedged. "He's authoritative, patient, the right amount of stern and kind. But he considers himself very forward-thinking, and part of his 'innovative' mentality is that the stuff we're teaching kids today isn't relevant for later life. We teach them the names of dead presidents, Pythagoras's theorem, and the taxonomic rank—"

"The what now?"

"You know." She rolled her finger. "Kingdom, phylum, class, order. I guess the fact that you don't know sort of proves his point. But as a science teacher . . ." Olive mimed driving a stake into her heart.

"But he still lets you teach that stuff, right?" Carter clarified.

"He has to. It's part of the core state curriculum. But he controls the budget, specifically discretionary funds that come in from any donations, etcetera. And let's just say our computer lab is state of the art, but the biology classroom is using the same microscopes and dissection kits we had when we were in high school."

"I take it you've asked for an upgrade to no avail?"

"Yup." She took a gulp of wine. "He says 99.9 percent of those kids won't need to know how to wield a scalpel or how to define *mitosis*. And of course, he's right, but what about that 0.1 percent that wants to be a doctor, or researcher, or cure freaking cancer?"

"Principal Mullins sounds like a shortsighted dunce," Carter said.

She clinked her glass against his. "I'm liking you more and more. Maybe."

He smiled. Not his usual megawatt smile, but a quieter, private smile, just for her. "I like you, too. Maybe."

Olive's stupid heart could handle the smile, but combined with the *I like you*, it left her distinctly . . . something.

"C'mon," he said, grabbing her glass out of her hand, and moving toward the kitchen. "I think I've had just enough wine to start bossing you around on this invitation-mailing task."

"Oh! Right." Olive jumped to her feet, glad for the reminder. She'd do well to remember that Carter Ramsey's presence in her life was purposeful, and very, very temporary.

Chapter Ten

There were two coffee shops in town.

One was a year and a half old and had a fireplace, comfy seating, a variety of carefully selected roasts from around the world, and seasonal delights that rivaled Starbucks.

The other was older than Olive, had wobbly tables and hard metal chairs, was chronically five degrees too warm, and generally offered only watery drip coffee when the espresso machine was "acting up," which was often. It was also owned and run by SherryLee Mullins, who had inherited it from her mother and, most importantly at the moment, was married to Principal Mullins—Olive's boss.

Which meant that when choosing which coffee shop to patronize, Olive winced through the tepid sludge at SherryLee's rather than cozying up with a mint fudge mocha at Rollie's Roasters.

It was good old-fashioned ass-kissing, and Olive would never have done it on behalf of herself. But if charming Mrs. Mullins meant she'd put in a good word with her husband, which in turn meant Olive could get better lab equipment for her students?

For that, Olive would smooch booty all day long.

Unfortunately, Mrs. Mullins had thus far proven herself impervious to Olive's special kind of charm. And since she really needed to win over the Mullinses for reasons that had nothing to do with her classroom, she didn't feel the least bit guilty about employing the big guns.

Or at least, that was the plan. Her big gun was ten minutes late.

The tinkle of the bell signaled that the Man of the Year had finally decided to grace her with his presence, and she gave Carter a glare generally reserved for tardy students.

"Sorry, Teach," he said with a grin, extending a long leg to pull out the chair with his sneaker. He swung a leg over it, sitting on it backward, good arm braced on the back of the chair.

Olive gave him a look. "Cool move. Will the rest of the T-Birds be joining us?"

"It is a cool move."

"Well, *un*-cool it," Olive said, lowering her voice. "Before *she* comes back and sees you."

"Before who—"

"Young man, that is not how a gentleman sits with a lady," SherryLee said, coming out from the back room with a bakery box in hand. She wasn't a day over forty-five but seemed to relish acting twice her age. Or at the very least, she took great delight in making anyone who came into her orbit feel nine years old.

"Good thing I'm not in the presence of a lady, then," Carter muttered under his breath, as he righted the chair.

"Rude," Olive said.

"Really? I watched you down an entire Gatorade in three gulps yesterday, and do not try to pretend that burp wasn't you."

"I needed to replenish my electrolytes after the hell you put me through."

"We played catch in your front yard. Which I still maintain doesn't count toward one of our five baseball sessions."

"It counts," Olive said decisively. "It was a full ten minutes."

"Yes, but you caught only ten percent of the balls, so . . ."

"Here you are, Olivia," SherryLee said, coming over and setting a tired-looking latte in front of her.

"It's Olive."

SherryLee wrinkled her nose. "Which I presume is short for Olivia."

"Nope. Parents were just big fans of Popeye," Olive explained, and not for the first time.

"Hmm." SherryLee's eyebrows crept up toward her teased blonde bangs. "Well, *Olive*, I made the latte with regular, as you insisted, but let's switch to decaf next time."

"Why?" Olive couldn't help asking. She'd never been particularly good at the ass-kissing game.

"When I was pregnant with my two boys, I wouldn't think of touching caffeine."

Olive pressed her lips together. Both of SherryLee's sons had come through Olive's class in the past couple of years, and they were not exactly the cream of Haven's crop in terms of personality. A little caffeine in the womb could only have helped, in Olive's nonexpert medical opinion. And even more to the point . . .

"I'm not pregnant," Olive said.

"Not yet. But that caffeine will build up in your system."

Olive was just about to point out that that was not how caffeine worked, when SherryLee mercifully shifted her judgmental gaze to Carter.

"Young man, it's not polite to wear hats indoors at a nice establishment."

Carter dutifully removed his Hawks cap, running his hand through his short hair and giving SherryLee a sheepish grin.

Yesssssss, Olive thought with glee. That's the stuff. *Reel her in, Big Gun!*

The coffee shop owner's blue eyes widened slightly. "Why, as I live and breathe, it's Carter Ramsey!"

Olive gave in to the urge to roll her eyes, since SherryLee wasn't looking at her anyway. *As I live and breathe?* You'd think SherryLee was born on the set of *Gone with the Wind* instead of in New York State.

"I'd heard you were back in town," SherryLee said, cocking her hip to one side and planting a fist on it. "Shame about the injury. Kirk and I don't miss a game, but it's just not the same without your good-looking face gracing our TV screen."

"Appreciate that, ma'am," Carter said, letting a deferential note enter his tone. He was *good* at this.

"What brings you into my shop?" SherryLee asked. The dubious glance in Olive's direction asked the real question: Why are you here with her?

"Just connecting with old . . . friends." Carter answered SherryLee's question, but his eyes were on Olive as he said it, and she sucked in a breath in response to the heated gaze.

Her brain knew he was messing with the nosy SherryLee, but her body was suddenly very aware that this man had been named the sexiest man in the country with good reason.

"I see," SherryLee said, skepticism clearly warring with excitement over a juicy morsel of gossip. "Can I get you something to drink?"

"Whatever Olive's having sounds great," Carter said, still not looking away from Olive.

"Are you sure?" Olive said in a scandalized whisper, after SherryLee slowly walked away, lingering with the hope of catching any of their conversation. "It has *caffeine*."

"I'll take my chances."

"You know, with the steamy look you just lit me on fire with, she's going to think it's your imaginary babies I'm threatening with my latte."

"Don't worry. I'll make an honest woman of you, Dunn."

"I'll need a ring first. My daddy always told me that no boy would buy the cow when he could have the milk for free."

"Did he?" Carter asked curiously.

Olive laughed. "Definitely not. His idea of the birds-and-the-bees talk was to tell me to read *On the Origin of Species* and *Gray's Anatomy*. I was eleven."

"My mom told me about his passing. I'm sorry."

She shrugged, even though the lance of pain felt surprisingly fresh, given it had been nearly three years. "We've all got to say goodbye to someone sometime, right? I mean, I'll never understand how a man that smart never kicked his three-pack-a-day habit, but alas. Besides, he wouldn't have liked you."

Carter shook his head. "Everybody likes me."

"Dad wouldn't have. Or rather, I don't think he'd have noticed you. He was sort of the brainy, aloof type."

"So he wouldn't have been happy about me knocking you up?"

"No. I do wish he could have met his grandchildren, though," Olive said a little wistfully.

"So babies are a part of your future?" he asked.

"I hope so. I want kids. In a perfect world, I'd have them the old-fashioned way. True love, husband, babies. Preferably in that order. But I'm also practical. If that doesn't happen, I can adopt or go the sperm-donor route." She batted her eyelashes at him. "I don't suppose your tadpoles are available. I'd just *love* to raise the next Babe Ruth."

"Based on what I've seen of your hand-eye coordination, no child of ours would stand a chance at athletic superstardom, even with my superb genes trying to get their say."

"Which means they'd be well-rounded delights. Just like me."

"Oh, well in that case, when do we get started?"

"Don't get excited," she said. "This would be a strictly *dirty magazine, your little soldiers into a cup and frozen* situation, no bumping your uglies up on mine."

"There you go again, adding a touch of gentle sensuality to everything."

Olive beamed at him, then took a sip of her coffee and winced.

"What's wrong?"

"Nothing." She pushed the mug away. "You'd think that one of these days I'd learn that the coffee here is always lukewarm at best."

"So why are we here?"

"Because SherryLee is married to Principal Mullins. Normally, I'm here in a futile attempt to sweet-talk her into sweet-talking him into getting new microscopes. Today, however, we have a different mission."

"Convincing her to be godmother to our children?"

"Way more difficult. We need the gym."

"Come again?"

"Reunion business, son," Olive said, making a posturing gesture. "Did you really think I'd toss that dumb ball around with you last night—"

"*Toss* is a strong word for what you were doing."

"Shush. It's quid pro quo time. We're here to convince SherryLee to convince Kirk to let us use the gym for the reunion. For free."

"Isn't that pretty standard protocol for high school reunions? I don't see why we have to drink shitty coffee in order to do that. Can't we just ask?"

"Says the guy who's been gone ten years. You missed the debacle that was Haven High's twenty-year reunion a couple years ago."

"What happened?"

"Let's just say that Generation X's partying skills are no joke. For the first two months of that school year, our sports teams had to use the Wilton District's gym for practice while the fire damage to our gym was repaired."

"Fire damage. That's impressive. And alarming."

"Indeed. Principal Mullins banned all future reunions from happening on school premises, because *that's* the reasonable reaction. Last year's ten-year reunion team had to put a big tent on the football field, which of course paired really nicely with the late-summer thunderstorm."

"What about the fancy golf club?"

"Oh yeah. We totally have the budget for that. Right along with the caviar and imported champagne," Olive said.

"I'm so excited to raise our sarcastic children."

"Children?" SherryLee chirped, setting a latte in front of Carter that had perfect-looking foam, the likes of which Olive had never seen come from SherryLee's espresso machine, as well as honest-to-goodness steam.

"This is perfect. Thank you so much, Mrs. Mullins," Carter said with a wide smile. "Say, I was wondering if you could help me with something. I don't get back to Haven nearly as much as I like to, which is a shame, because it's full of so many great memories for me, especially at the high school. In fact, I was just telling Olive here, I can't believe it's been a full ten years since I've been inside the gym . . ."

Olive smiled and reached across the table, pulling Carter's much hotter, much more delicious latte toward her, taking a sip as she let Carter work his Man of the Year magic.

Less than five minutes later, SherryLee was calling her husband. Less than one minute after that, Principal Mullins agreed to let Haven High's ten-year reunion happen in the high school gym.

"What do you know?" Olive said happily, as they stepped out into the humid summer weather a few minutes later. "Being friends with Carter Ramsey has its perks after all."

"Remember that tonight."

"What's tonight?" she asked.

"Scorekeeping," he said, grinning down at her. "Tracking every single pitch, hit, and error of an entire MLB game."

Olive made a pained noise. "All nine periods?"

"Innings," he clarified with a laugh.

"Right. How long will that last?"

Carter dropped his arm over her shoulders as they walked toward their cars. "About three hours. Three long, glorious hours, future mother of my children."

Olive groaned dramatically.

Anything to keep him from discovering that she was actually looking forward to it.

Chapter Eleven

Olive was busy comparing the unit price on bulk toilet paper at Walmart when she was enveloped with a wonderfully familiar vanilla scent, followed immediately by someone soft and warm hugging her from behind.

"You're back!" Olive said, knowing who it was even before she turned around to return the enthusiastic hug.

Sofia Castiano was a substitute teacher at Haven High, and one of Olive's closest friends. She and her husband had been in Puerto Rico for the past couple of weeks visiting family, and Olive had forgotten that she was due back.

"Oh my gosh, I kid you not, I was just about to text you and see if you had time for lunch next week when I looked up, and what did I see but you standing right in front of me, going to town on toilet paper."

"Um, can we not phrase it that way?" Olive said, grabbing a double ply that promised to be soft and strong and dropping it into her basket. "When did you get back? How was it? I want to know everything."

"Oh, you know," Sofia said with a dramatic sigh, resting her forearms on the handle of her cart, her trademark high bun waggling atop her head. "Both sides of the family think we've completely and irrevocably screwed up the boys' lives. Luis's family thinks it's my fault for daring to want a career, and my mother can't go five minutes without pointing out that Luis's mother skipped mass once, eight months ago."

"So, typical family stuff?" Olive asked.

"Exactly. I was like, 'Ohmigod, I love you guys so much, but also you might kill me.' Anyway, it's good to be back, especially since . . ." Sofia nudged her cart closer and lowered her voice to a loud whisper, even though they had the toilet paper aisle all to themselves. "Have you heard?"

"Probably," Olive said confidently. "That Carol Ann is having triplets? False, it's twins. Girls. That Bob and Brenda Hamlin separated? Sadly, true. That we're getting a Chipotle where that weird carpet store used to be? Tragically, false. Though—"

"Oh my God, Olive, *Chipotle*, Olive? Who cares! I'm talking about the fact that Carter Ramsey is here in Haven."

"Oh," Olive said with a little smile. "Yeah. Actually—"

"And," Sofia continued excitedly, "have you heard *why* he's here?"

"Sure. The reunion, and his family—"

"Felicity George," Sofia said triumphantly.

Olive blinked. "What?"

"Felicity George," Sofia repeated, blinking her wide brown eyes in puzzlement at Olive. "I didn't move to Haven until after she'd left, but I thought for sure that you'd know who—"

"I know who she is," Olive said, sorting through her thoughts. Of course she knew her. Next to Carter, she was one of Haven's more famous residents, though more by association to her Hollywood director husband. Come to think of it, she wasn't Felicity George anymore. She'd become Felicity Alpert since marrying Todd Alpert, best known for directing a teen TV series about witches, or warlocks, or magicians, or something. Olive had never seen it. She actually hadn't spent much mental energy on Felicity George . . . ever.

In high school, they hadn't been friends or run in the same circles. Even when Felicity had been in Olive's senior government group, they'd sort of coexisted without really connecting. Not enemies, just indifferent to each other.

Carter, on the other hand, had not been indifferent to Felicity George. Quite the opposite.

Olive swallowed, alarmed by how bothered she was at the thought that Carter was here in Haven to see Felicity. She shouldn't be. The day Carter moved in next door, it had been her first thought. She'd assumed that *of course* there was a connection between his reappearance and Felicity's newly single status.

But then she'd gotten to know Carter, and she'd quit thinking about Felicity altogether.

And Carter hadn't mentioned his ex.

His omission was telling. Olive just wasn't entirely sure what it said.

"The part about Carter is true," Olive said slowly. "He is back. But I don't know about Felicity. She hasn't RSVPed to the reunion, so it could be conjecture."

"Nope," Sofia said confidently. "Oh my gosh, I can't believe I know something you don't. Anna Russel stopped by last night to borrow some carpet cleaner after her cat puked in her living room, and she told me that she heard from Felicity's cousin's wife at Pilates that Felicity is for sure coming to town to attend the reunion and reconnect with people."

"Huh." Olive began pushing her cart toward the front of the store, pretending indifference to the news. Which was annoying. She shouldn't have to pretend to be indifferent; she should actually be indifferent. Who cared if gorgeous, petite, universally popular Felicity wanted to come back for the reunion? The more the merrier.

What was it to Olive if the person Felicity likely most wanted to reconnect with was Olive's temporary neighbor?

What did it matter if that neighbor hadn't mentioned Felicity to Olive?

No big, said her brain.

Wtf, said her heart.

"So, have you seen him?" Sofia said, falling into step with Olive, pushing her cart beside hers.

Olive didn't pretend not to know who *him* was in reference to. "Actually, yeah. He's helping me plan the reunion."

"What?" Sofia halted, then reached out to snag a finger in one of the holes of Olive's cart, pulling her to a stop as well. "You and Carter Ramsey are friends?"

"Well, no. I'm friends with Caitlyn, who's supposed to be helping plan the reunion, but she's on bed rest, and—anyway, it kind of became a whole thing."

"What kind of thing?" Sofia said, her eyes wide and fascinated.

"Not the kind of thing you're thinking," Olive said, gently extracting her friend's hand from her cart and pushing forward again. "We're just neighbors."

"Neighbors!" Sofia squeaked. "How could you not have texted me all this? I leave for two weeks, and I come back to my work bestie shacking up with a celebrity. Did you know his contract with the Hawks is one of the largest in MLB history? Like, lots of zeros. Luis said the team could lose millions if he doesn't get better after his injury—okay, whatever, who cares. Is he as hot as he seems on TV?"

Olive pointed at the checkout stand as they neared the front of the store. "You done shopping? I'm ready to check out."

"Ugh, no, I've barely dented my list," Sofia said. "But for real, before I go buy frozen pizza in bulk, you've got to give me something. Is Carter hot, or does his baseball cap just disguise his flaws on TV? Is he conceited? Short? I've always heard that celebs are shorter in real life than you think."

"He's good-looking. Cocky, definitely, but not a jerk about it. And he's got several inches on me."

"Ooh, so tall," Sofia said reverently. "And hot."

"I said good-looking," Olive pointed out.

"Yes, but if *you* think someone is good-looking, it means he's hot. Just like when you were dating that math teacher from Woodstock and said he was 'interesting looking,' you failed to mention the unfortunate way his huge nose emphasized his lack of chin."

"Kenneth was sweet," Olive protested. "And smart. And kind."

"I know. And yet, you're no longer seeing him because . . ."

"Long distance," Olive replied instantly.

"Annnnnd?" Sofia prompted.

"I never should have told you," Olive muttered.

"He refused to be on top during scx." Sofia paired a dismissive *pttttthhd* noise with a thumbs-down.

Olive shrugged. Sex with Kenneth had been disappointing, but then, in Olive's experience, sex in general was disappointing. Pleasant, definitely, but there was nothing earth-shattering about it.

"I'll bet Carter Ramsey doesn't mind being on top," Sofia said, slowly fanning herself. "Or on the bottom. Or standing up. Or—"

"Stop." Olive held up a hand. "He's my neighbor and, weirdly, sort of my friend. I don't want to think about him having sex."

And she certainly didn't want to think about him having sex with Felicity George.

◆　◆　◆

"Admit it," Carter said, finishing the rest of his sparkling water, then crumpling the can in his fist. "It was sort of satisfying."

Olive took her time responding, lifting the official MLB scoring sheet that she'd just completed. Carter had had one of the team's PAs overnight him one, and he and Olive had spent the last three hours watching the Hawks play as she had gamely kept score with his instruction.

"People do this with every game? For fun?"

Carter shrugged. "Sure."

Olive continued to study her tidy score sheet, then gave a smug smile. "I'm putting this on my refrigerator."

He smiled. "So you did have fun."

"Don't get riled up. I will never do it again," she said, setting the scorecard on the table and picking up her mug of tea. "But as a onetime exercise in understanding baseball, it was quite useful."

"Thought you might appreciate the academic side of the sport."

"I do," she admitted. "I didn't even mind when it went into the tenth interval."

"*Inning*, Olive. Good God, was that a wasted three hours?"

She grinned, and he rolled his eyes when he realized she'd been baiting him.

"I wonder if Principal Mullins would let me be the official score-keeper at the softball game next weekend rather than actually play," she mused.

"Oh right, Caitlyn mentioned something about that. There really is a softball game?"

"Every August," she said with a dramatic sigh. "I could sort of understand if it was just a 'for fun' way to hang out with teachers from other districts, but people get way into it. Last year, Principal Mullins tried to bribe us all into playing our best by saying whomever he named the MVP moved to the top of the list for a new laptop."

Carter hadn't seen Olive's laptop, but he'd seen her inability to catch a softball. It went without saying that she hadn't been the MVP.

"What's the bribe this year?"

"No clue. But there's literally no carrot he could dangle in front of my nose that would get me excited about that game."

"Not even new microscopes for your class?"

"Okay, that, yes," Olive said, pointing at him. "I'd join a softball league for that. I'd become your ball girl for that—ooh, sex pun! But anyway, it's not going to happen. That's big money the district doesn't have. Or at least, big money the softball-obsessed Mullins wouldn't attach to a game."

Carter nodded, propping his feet up on Olive's ottoman. He'd originally planned for them to watch the game at his rented place, but she'd pointed out that hers was more comfortable, and she was right. His had all the standard furniture pieces in all the right places, but everything had a generic, beige sort of feel, as though someone had called a furniture superstore and told them to send "whatever."

Her home was warm, one of a kind, and comfortable.

Much like the woman herself.

Though she hadn't been herself tonight, at least not the Olive he'd come to know over the past week—strange, that it had been only that long when he felt as though this woman knew him as well as anyone, and he was coming to know her as well.

It was how he knew that even though she smiled, laughed, and bossed, there was something on her mind. Her smile dropped just a little more quickly, and there'd been a slight frown on her face whenever she'd thought he wasn't watching her. Strangely, he'd found Olive more interesting to watch than the game.

She was simply so alive, even when she was sitting perfectly still.

"You want to talk about it?" he asked her.

"'Bout what?" She looked at him over her mug, which she cupped with both hands.

"You seem preoccupied, and I know it's not because you're still thinking about the fielder's choice in the fourth inning."

"I still don't get it. He hit the ball. He got to first base safely. So why wasn't it a hit?"

"Because," Carter explained patiently, not for the first time, "he would have been out had there not been a runner on second, and had the shortstop not chosen to get the out at third instead."

"We can't know that. What if the shortstop would have thrown it to first, and the first baseman would have missed it?"

"Then he'd be on base by an error, which is still not a hit."

"I see."

He narrowed his eyes. "You're going to change it on the scorecard after I leave, aren't you?"

She gave him a wide smile, showing him all her teeth. Her eyes, though . . . they still didn't light all the way.

"That's not what's bothering you," he said.

"Jeez, you have to be athletic, good-looking, and perceptive?" she said grumpily, setting her mug back on the table, then sitting back on the couch, leg tucked beneath her as she turned to face him. "You really want to know?"

"Nope, just asked about it twice in hopes that you wouldn't tell me," Carter said.

"All right then, here it is," she said, gesturing with her hand as though to say, *you asked for it.* "Are you here in Haven because Felicity George is coming back to town?"

Carter went still. He didn't know precisely what had been bothering Olive, but he'd assumed it'd be related to her job, her boss, the reunion, or maybe something she'd heard around town, because as far as he could tell, she seemed to know everyone and everything.

Which was why it should have occurred to him that the woman who knew everything would also know that.

"I heard a few days before you got into town that Felicity was divorced and maybe coming back. But all this time, you've never mentioned it. Weren't you like really *serious* with her?"

Carter exhaled. "It's not like it's a big secret." He deliberately didn't answer the part about being serious with Felicity. He had been. But discussing it with Olive felt strange.

Especially since in the past couple of days, he'd been thinking a lot more about Olive than he had Felicity.

"Okay, so, she is coming to town," Olive said slowly. "When?"

"I don't know."

"She hasn't booked her flight yet?"

"I have no idea. I haven't talked to her."

"Since—when?"

"Since ten years ago," he said with a tight smile.

Olive's mouth dropped open. "Seriously?"

"Do you go around talking to a lot of your exes?" Suddenly, he was more than a little curious about her exes.

"Well, no," she admitted. "But I also don't rent a house with the expectation of seeing them, and then not get in touch. What's the big plan? You're just going to bump into her at Cedar & Salt?"

He winced.

Olive rolled her eyes. "Oh good God. That was your plan?"

It had been his plan. Now, he had to admit, he hadn't thought about Felicity much at all, considering she was the primary reason he'd returned to Haven. He still wanted to see her. Eventually. But not in the urgent, hopeful way he had when he'd first decided to come into town. Now, it was more of a passive curiosity. There was still a whisper of *what-if*, but there was no burn to it.

A week ago, the prospect of reuniting with Felicity had seemed far-fetched, but feasible. Desperate, yes, but also . . . practical. Now, he didn't want practical.

He sighed. "Look, between helping you plan the reunion, getting you to admit you were wrong about my job being hard, seeing my family, and staying in shape, there just hasn't been much time to go chasing down my ex," he told Olive.

"Bullshit," Olive said bluntly. "You're terrified to see her."

"I dated her for a year. Why would I be terrified?"

"I haven't the foggiest. But I do know that if you want something, you go after it. You don't become one of the highest-paid baseball players in history by sitting around and letting stuff come to you. If you wanted to get in touch with Felicity, you'd be in touch with Felicity. So, what's up?"

He glared at her. "You're annoying."

"I'm *right*."

Yeah. Yeah, she was right.

Irritably, he adjusted the strap of his sling, stalling for time as he marveled at the fact that he had never told his mother, his twin, or any of his friends what had gone down with Felicity a decade ago, and somehow he was considering telling Olive Dunn.

No. He *wanted* to tell Olive Dunn.

"All right," he muttered. "But this stays between us."

"Oh, I don't like secrets," she said bluntly.

"But you'll keep one if I ask," he said with confidence.

She hesitated, then nodded. "Sure. Absolutely I will."

He took a deep breath. "Felicity and I were good together. We only dated for a year, but it was a damn good year, and I loved her."

Olive nodded. "I know. Lab partner, remember? You wrote her gushy notes."

He winced. "You knew about that?"

She gave him a look.

"Right," he said with a laugh. "Olive Dunn knows everything. But not this."

"Ooh!" Her eyes widened. "Intrigue."

"Sure. Okay, so, we cared about each other, but I was also eighteen. I'd spent the past couple months stressed about whether to play college ball at Florida State or go pro. Her parents had been counting the days until graduation so they could move to California to be near her grandparents, and she'd been accepted to—and enrolled in—a school out there."

"You guys had planned to do long distance?"

"To be honest, I hadn't planned much of anything," Carter said, leaning forward and looking down at his feet. "I'd been sort of putting off the decision, figuring that what was meant to be would be. Then, in . . . July, I guess it was, she came over to my place all excited to tell me she wasn't going to go to college in California after all."

"Where was she going to go?"

Carter looked up. "With me, apparently. I'd been drafted by that point and was just waiting for my minor league assignment. She said us being together was the most important thing."

"You didn't agree?"

"I loved her," Carter said. "But . . . I told her to go to college. As planned."

"Good," Olive said emphatically.

He exhaled out a laugh. "It didn't feel that way at the time. But I knew it was the right thing—I didn't want her giving her life up for me until she'd really had a chance to build her own life."

"How'd she take it?"

"I don't think I've ever seen anyone cry that much," he admitted. "So, it sucked. Especially when she stopped crying long enough to tell me that she didn't want to do long distance. That she couldn't stomach the thought of being on the other side of the country not knowing what I was doing, or who I was sleeping with . . ."

"Oooh boy."

"Yeah. She left, pissed, and I thought we were done."

Olive was listening attentively. "Is this where the intriguing part comes in?"

He nodded. "The next day, she showed up again. Calmer. Weirdly calm, I thought. She told me that she loved me, would always love me, but that she understood our lives were taking us in different directions."

Olive sighed and picked up her tea. "I don't mean to be rude, but this isn't all that interesting. I thought she was at least going to throw a baseball at you. Now that would make a good story."

"Well, maybe if you quit interrupting," he grumbled. Then he gave her the part of the story he hadn't told a soul: "Felicity suggested that we part ways, amicably. But if in ten years, neither of us were married, that we would . . ." He broke off and finished the rest on a mutter. "That we would marry each other."

He finally brought himself to look at Olive, whose eyes were comically wide. "Please tell me you didn't agree to that."

He winced.

"You did!" Olive said with a delighted laugh. "Oh my God. Oh my God! That is too good. I didn't know that sort of thing happened outside of terrible movies! A marriage pact!"

"I was eighteen," he said under his breath. "And I'd already hurt her. I didn't want her to start crying again, and—"

"And?" she managed through a laugh, wiping her eyes.

"Well, honestly, I thought I'd be married by now! And she married the Hollywood guy, so I chalked the whole thing up to childhood crap and forgot about it."

"Until you found out she was divorced," Olive said. "And going to be a two-hour drive away from your place in the city."

He paused a moment, then gave a single nod.

Olive's laughter slowly died. "Wait. Carter. You aren't seriously thinking . . . It's one thing to make a stupid pact when you're eighteen and don't know any better. But you're twenty-eight now."

"Exactly. It's been ten years. I'm single. And she's single."

"And you haven't seen or talked to each other in all that time! You won't even call her!"

"You don't get it," he snapped, standing abruptly and pacing irritably around her living room.

"No, I don't. But explain it to me," Olive said slowly.

"The timing of it . . . rocked me, a little. I've been so preoccupied with my identity as a baseball player for so long. Then this happened." He lifted his broken arm slightly. "And all of a sudden, I realized I don't know who I am. Or what I am. And I guess I wanted to remember what it was like to be liked before I became what I am now."

"An über-famous multimillionaire?"

He nodded. "And the girl who loved me before I was all of that seemed like a good person to help me figure it out."

"So, let me get this straight," she said, leaning her elbows on her knees and studying him. "You've spent the past decade making oodles of money because you happen to have really good hand-eye coordination. Your face is about to be plastered all over a magazine cover because your features happen to be arranged in a semipleasing manner, and you're saying you want to go back to . . . before all that?"

He gave a half smile. "Semipleasing manner?"

"We don't have time for compliment fishing right now."

"We don't?"

"No." She shook her head. "We're in problem-solving mode."

His smile faded entirely. "Some problems you can't fix."

Olive scowled. "All problems can be fixed."

He shook his head and was beyond annoyed to realize he had a frustrated lump in his throat.

Olive's face scrunched in concern; then her gaze dropped to his sling, and he saw the moment she understood. "I thought—I googled it. It was a clean break. You said you'd get the cast off in four to six weeks."

"It was. I will." He pinched the bridge of his nose, and before he realized what he was doing, he was dropping his other bomb on Olive Dunn. "I've got a SLAP tear. In my left shoulder."

"A what now?"

"A superior labral tear from anterior to posterior." Carter's voice had a terse precision as he said the words he'd gotten all too familiar with. "Basically, a kiss-of-death injury for someone who has to throw for a living. It's more detrimental for pitchers, but no peach for the rest of us, either."

"Is it from the same fall?"

He shook his head. "It'd been bothering me for a couple weeks before my arm injury. I thought it was just some tightness, that I'd sprained it a bit. But when they were scanning my arm after the fall, they found the tear in my shoulder, too."

"What does it mean?" she asked calmly.

"A broken forearm's a for-sure return to play. A SLAP tear's a probable return to play. Even the combination . . . I'll get back on the field. But a return to elite performance? I'll never be as good as I was."

"How come nobody's talking about the shoulder, if that's the worse one?"

Carter gave a half smile. "Nobody knows. Just you, my agent, and the doctor. Not my teammates, not the press, not even my family."

Olive absorbed this information slowly, then nodded and stood. "I feel like I should warn you, I've never really hugged a man other than my dad before. Not in a platonic way."

"Um, okay," he said, puzzled.

"So this will very likely be awkward for both of us," she said, walking toward him and unceremoniously winding her arms around his waist, careful not to jar his broken arm.

She was wrong. Carter instinctively put his good arm around her and pulled her as close as he could. It wasn't awkward.

It was exactly what he needed.

Chapter Twelve

"Why did you kidnap me again?"

"It's called carpooling," Olive explained patiently. "We're going to the same place, and because I know you love the planet as much as I do, we're doing our part to limit fuel emissions. I'd have suggested riding bikes, but I don't have one for you."

"Damn, too bad," he said. "Would have been pretty great to break my *other* arm."

She shot him a look. "How's that?"

"Let's just say it's been a while since I've ridden a bike," he said, turning his head to look out the window and seeming more pensive than usual.

"You ride the stationary ones in the gym, and you had that fancy bike machine installed in the living room of your rental house like a weirdo."

"It's a little different when it's a machine that stays immobile on the floor versus tearing around town like I'm a twelve-year-old kid from *The Goonies*."

"You're obviously not twelve years old if you're making a *Goonies* reference. That movie is older than you are."

"Don't mock the classics, Dunn," he said with a quick grin. "But thanks for the reminder that I'm a young buck."

She smiled back, though she knew there was more to his comment than a casual quip. She knew it ate at him that his career had an expiration date. She wished she knew how to help. It had been several days since he'd told her the truth about the extent of his injuries, and Olive was a bit miffed to realize that no matter how much she thought about it, no matter how hard she brainstormed, this was one thing she couldn't fix.

But.

While she may not be able to fix his arm, she could at least keep his brain distracted. From his shoulder. From his cast. From freaking Felicity George, who Olive had learned would be getting into town sometime over the weekend.

Not that Olive had told Carter about Felicity's impending arrival. If he wanted to reconnect with his old girlfriend, that was his business. If he wanted to follow through with their decade-old pact, that was lunacy, but also his business.

She couldn't—*wouldn't*—tell him how to conduct his personal life, but Olive was going to at least do her part to make sure Carter Ramsey's head was on as straight as it possibly could be before he made any sort of weird, hasty decisions influenced by his uncertain career future.

A marriage pact.

For God's sake.

It was as ridiculous now as when he'd first told her about it, but the more she thought about it, the more she understood why it had brought him back to Haven in the first place. For a guy who was facing the possible end of his career with no idea what came next, maybe it made sense to look backward for comfort. For Carter, comfort meant Felicity.

Alarmingly, Olive was becoming increasingly worried that *her* source of comfort was Carter. Which would be all fine and dandy if he didn't have plans to leave town the second he got his cast removed.

Felicity very well might be willing to follow him when he left, but Olive belonged here, in Haven.

"Here we are!" Olive said, forcing brightness into her tone as she pulled into the deserted Haven High faculty parking lot. "Ready to get inspired for our reunion theme? We've got less than three weeks to go and zero ideas."

"And being here will help us how?" Carter asked, climbing out of the car.

"It probably won't," she admitted, shutting the car door behind her. "But I've got to take some measurements in the gym to figure out what size tables to rent, and I figured it'd give you a chance to bask in your old glory days."

She gestured for him to go frolic, but instead of moving, he glanced at her curiously. "Is it weird?"

"Is what weird?" Olive asked.

"Working in the same building where your teenage self suffered through puberty?"

Olive's tone was sharper than she meant it to be when she replied. "We can't all rush off to the land of the rich and famous after graduation, and some of us don't want to. There's nothing wrong with staying in your hometown."

He blinked in surprise. "Of course there's not. That's not what I meant."

"I know," she said quietly, not quite looking at him. "It's just that I *like* my job. I don't feel I should have to defend it just because I don't make millions of dollars and get my face plastered on a magazine."

"Ouch." He said it softly, and with a slight smile, but he looked stung and rightfully so. She knew she was one of the few people— maybe the only person—he'd trusted enough to share his Man of the Year secret with, and she was throwing it in his face.

She winced. "I'm sorry. That was bitchy."

"Forgiven. Though will you bite my head off if I say you're not exactly acting like yourself?"

"No," Olive said with a weary exhale. "You're right."

"What's up?" he asked, looking both curious and concerned.

Olive wished she knew. Ever since finding out Carter had come back to Haven for Felicity, she'd felt off-balance. Here she'd thought they were building an actual friendship, and now she couldn't shake the sense that she was just a placeholder to keep him entertained until the love of his life showed up.

"Nothing," she lied. "Just a good old-fashioned *woke up on the wrong side of the bed* situation. Don't worry, I'll snap out of it. Now, where were we? I believe you were busy judging my life decisions?"

He made a sound of irritation. "Damn it, woman, I wasn't judging you. I think it's great that you like your job."

"I do," she said, trying to shove away her cranky mood. "I *really* love it. Education's so important, and yet so often people treat it as some sort of mundane, youthful obligation to be checked off before real life begins."

He turned in a wide circle as he walked, taking in their old high school campus. "Little do they know some of their best days will be here," he said, shoving his hand in his pocket and looking up at the building.

Olive sneaked a glance at him as she dug her keys out of her purse, wondering if he was thinking about Felicity, then shook her head. Of course he was. His baseball career had only exploded since he left high school. But his romantic life, from what Google had told her in her shameless online stalking over the past couple of days, had apparently peaked in high school.

Perhaps not for long, though. Not if he and Felicity picked up where they'd left off.

She pushed away the thought as she shoved open the door to the main administration building, then used the key once again, this time to turn on the master lights.

They flickered on, noisy and fluorescent, and Carter grinned as he looked around. "Wow. It looks exactly the same."

"Not much has changed," Olive agreed. "They repainted the walls a couple years ago, and the computer lab is state of the art. But there's not much money left over to completely scrub the *seventies* off the place."

"Holy crap." He halted and pointed to his left, at a bright blue locker that looked like every other bright blue locker. "That's my locker. My exact locker."

"You sound upset. Were you expecting it to be turned into a shrine?"

"Not upset. Just . . . It's weird," he murmured, setting a hand to it, a small smile on his lips, as though lost in memories.

She looked away, because he had the same wistful look again, and she was completely certain he wasn't reminiscing about time spent with his weird lab partner. Not when he had the pristine memory of Felicity George. Olive had no distinct memories of Carter and Felicity together in high school, just a vague recollection that they'd been a couple. She hadn't given much thought to their relationship then, and she certainly hadn't given much thought to it over the past decade, but . . . she was thinking about it now. Imagining a pretty, smiley Felicity leaning back against Carter's locker. Imagining Carter leaning down to sneak a kiss when teachers weren't around.

Imagining that it was Olive who was smiling up at him, that *she* was the one he was kissing . . .

Nope. Olive caught herself before the disastrous fantasy could go any further.

"Shut it down," she muttered to herself.

"What?"

"Nothing. Come on. Which of your old classrooms do you want to see?"

Olive showed him around the entire school, letting herself see Haven High through the eyes of someone who'd once ruled the school, and smiling a little at how genuinely happy he seemed.

"So what's next? The gym?"

"In a sec. I just need to swing by the supply room and pick up a couple poster boards. I want to put up a few more posters around town. It's cheesy, but it's for a high school reunion. It's supposed to be cheesy."

"More green glitter in your future?"

"I don't suppose *you* have any art skills? Then you could actually be useful in this reunion-planning thing," she said, opening the supply room closet and grabbing what she needed.

"Unfortunately, I've only got the one skill," he replied, dutifully using his good hand to hold the poster boards she handed up. "And for what it's worth, being famous is not all that it's cracked up to be."

"Hmm," she said. "Easier to say, probably, when you've had the luxury of experiencing it. Most people never even get the chance to reject fame, or muse about life before they were famous—" Olive broke off as inspiration hit hard.

"What?" Carter asked curiously.

"That's it," she said with a wide smile. "I'm a genius."

"There you go again, struggling with your confidence levels."

"Hush. Not everyone will get the opportunity to be famous, but everyone can *pretend* they turned out famous. Isn't that the cliché? To go to your high school reunion a celebrity with stories to tell?"

"Sure, I guess," he said skeptically. "Maybe in a *One Tree Hill* episode."

"You watched *One Tree Hill?*"

"I had a girlfriend who did, which, in high school, is sort of the same thing."

"Okay, whatever. We have our theme!" she said, clapping excitedly, her brain buzzing with ideas.

"What, *One Tree Hill?*" he asked.

"Ugh, no. Keep up. Our theme is 'Before They Were Famous.' Everyone can come dressed and in character of who they'd be if they were famous. We'll make it all fancy, lifestyles of the rich and famous, plus a little nostalgic when-they-were-young thing."

"Who would you be if you were famous?" he asked, following her as she headed toward the gym.

"Little old me? Why, I could *never* be famous," she said in a faux-breathy voice. "I'd be happy just being by the side of my famous baby daddy! He plays baseball!" She set a hand to her chest as she said it, batting her eyes dramatically at him, fully expecting him to roll his eyes in return.

Instead, he caught her gaze with his, and for one baffling moment, she could have sworn they were thinking the exact same thing: *What if?*

Chapter Thirteen

Wednesday, August 19

Carter glanced around the gym as the lights slowly flickered on, illuminating the familiar space. If the main admin building had brought back a rush of memories, the gym held a healthy dose of straight-up nostalgia.

Aside from the baseball field, which he hadn't seen yet, some of his favorite memories from high school had taken place in this ugly, smelly gym: PE classes, which had always been his favorites; tryouts for every sport had started here, and the flyer for who made what team had been posted here as well; school assemblies, which had always been a welcome break from class; high school dances, where the game of avoiding the chaperones had been nearly as rewarding as anything they played on the ball field.

It also smelled a bit like a gym bag that hadn't been cleaned in a long, long time.

"You sure this is the place?" he asked Olive, who was charging around with a tape measure.

"Unless you have a better idea and want your bewitching of SherryLee Mullins to be in vain."

"Had I known the price, I might not have tried so hard to apply my B-level charm on her," he said.

She glanced over. "That was B-level? What's your A-level?"

"You'll know it when you see it," he said, giving her a slow grin.

Olive, of course, looked unimpressed. "Was that it? I find myself distinctly uncharmed—zero chance of swooning."

"Have you ever swooned?"

"Of course not," she said, going back to her measuring.

For several minutes, there was nothing but the sound of her tape measure, followed by the sound of her pencil scratching across her notebook as she took notes. He would have asked what he could do to help, but he'd gotten to know this woman well enough to predict that the answer would be a big fat nothing. Olive didn't seem to need him—or anyone—for anything.

She'd been right when she'd told Caitlyn she didn't need a cochair. She was doing it just fine on her own. Still, he was strangely glad that he had agreed to help. If someone had told him that he'd be spending his August running around his hometown comparing the meatballs of two rival caterers and listening to his high school lab partner barter for a bulk discount on tulips, he'd have laughed in disbelief.

Yet here he was. Enjoying himself.

And not just because it was a distraction from his injury or from the fact that Felicity would be in town any day.

He was enjoying himself because he was enjoying . . .

Olive.

Carter shoved his hand into the pocket of his jeans and watched as she sat back on her haunches, chewing on the end of her pen, a little line of concentration between her brows. He'd thought maybe being back at the school would jog some more specific memories of Olive, but they remained fuzzy at best. All he remembered was a loud, opinionated girl who'd never pretended to be even remotely impressed by his high school popularity or the rumors that he'd be among the top draft picks after graduation.

His eyes drifted down over the utilitarian white shirt she was wearing that looked a lot like the shirts he had in his own closet. But he didn't wear them like she wore them. Didn't fill them out like that. His gaze drifted upward, over the long, no-nonsense ponytail pulled over one shoulder, the pink of her cheeks that he knew came from the sheer vitality of her, rather than makeup.

Her blue gaze lifted and collided with his, and for a moment, Carter felt downright disoriented.

"What?" she snapped.

He smiled, because just like that, he was reoriented.

And suddenly very curious.

"Why don't you have a boyfriend? Or girlfriend?" he asked, belatedly realizing just how little he knew about her romantic life.

"Who says I don't?" Olive looked back to her notebook and continued to scribble in it.

"You would have told me. Or I would have met them." He was pretty sure it wouldn't be a her—he'd caught her checking out his butt more than a few times.

"Well." She stood and stuck her pen behind her ear, continuing to survey the gym. "It's a small town. The pickings of men are a little slim for someone like me."

"Someone like you?" he asked, going to the lone set of bleachers not folded against the wall and sitting on the bottom bench.

She gave him a searching look. "Are you trying to bond? Why are you being weird?"

He merely grinned and patted the seat beside his. "Come. Don't be an enigma."

"Maybe I like being an enigma."

"Maybe," he agreed easily, though he knew it was crap. Olive Dunn was as *what you see is what you get* as they came.

"I'm not dainty," she said abruptly.

Or maybe not, Carter realized, backpedaling on his assumptions that he knew Olive well. He certainly hadn't seen that response coming.

"Dainty?" he repeated, the word unfamiliar on his tongue. "What's dainty got to do with anything?"

She gave him a *get real* look out of the corner of her eye. "Men like dainty, and don't pretend they don't. Even the men who profess a love for curvy, more-to-love women go crazy over things like little hands and feet."

"What the hell kind of men are you hanging out with? Where are you getting your information?"

"Magazines. TV. Personal experience."

He sat forward and turned his head toward where she remained seated on the gym floor. "Now we're getting somewhere."

"It's not like a whole thing," she said, sounding more flustered than he'd ever heard her. "I just mean that my longest relationship was a year, was tepid at best, and though I think the men I've dated like me well enough, I feel like that's all it's ever been. *Like.* Just reliable, clamp-on-the-shoulder, good ol' Olive."

He frowned. She was worthy of a hell of a lot better than that. "A lot of relationships start in friendship. Maybe they'd have grown to more than *like*."

She shrugged disinterestedly. "Maybe. Or maybe it's me. A couple years ago I had two back-to-back relationships where the guys left me for someone else. One fell for his coworker. The other got back together with his ex-girlfriend."

Olive paired that last bit of information with a telling look in his direction, but Carter ignored it, not even remotely interested in talking about Felicity right now. He wanted to know more about Olive, and this was a piece of the puzzle he hadn't had before.

"These other women. Were they . . . dainty?" he guessed.

"The secretary was a size zero. I know because I met her twice, and she mentioned it. Twice. As for the other one's ex, yeah, she was basically pocket-sized. I mean, I don't have a problem with petite women. They can't help their size any more than I can help mine. It's just they seem to have that elusive quality that makes people—men—want to take care of them. Men love that shit."

"Do we?" he murmured, thinking it over.

"Sure," she said, pushing to her feet and then coming to plop beside him, her thigh pressed against his with an easy, platonic comfortability that both pleased and annoyed him. Pleased, because he felt the same level of comfort around her. Annoyed, because he was thinking about what this woman looked like naked a little more every day, and as far as he could tell, she viewed him as a brother.

"I'm sure it's not a conscious thing," Olive said, oblivious to his sexual thoughts as ever. "It's just biology. The way lions are mostly matriarchal and yet it's generally the male lions, with their stockier builds, that protect their pride from intruders. Or the way—"

"Hold up there, Biology Teacher," he said, interrupting. "I'm sure you're right about the animal kingdom, but give us human males a little credit. I'd like to think we've evolved beyond guarding the group—"

"Pride. Or pack, if we're talking about wolves, or—"

"*But,*" he interrupted, gently but decisively speaking over her, because it was important that she hear this. "Real men—human men—don't necessarily want a little lady to protect."

"No?" she asked, sounding curious, and a bit amused. "What do you want?"

Carter opened his mouth to respond, fully prepared to put her in her place, to tell her she was wrong about men. About him. About herself.

No words came out. Did he even have a clue what he wanted?

And if he did know, was it even his to take?

Olive gave his knee a friendly pat as she stood. "Yeah. I thought so."

Chapter Fourteen

"Yup. Saturday, two o'clock. I've had it on my calendar, and . . . Oh. Oh, wow, okay, that's . . . Yep, I'll be there. I can't wait. See you then." Olive hung up the phone, then promptly pressed her forehead against the cool metal of her refrigerator with a long moan.

She had just made peace with her conscience over calling in "sick" for the Saturday softball game. She'd never in her entire career faked being sick to miss a school day, but for a "for fun" softball game? Olive had her faux cough perfected.

Now, however, the stakes had been raised. Sadly, not to new microscopes for her class. That would be a little too good to be true. But still, it was *something*. Principal Mullins had just called to tell her that the MVP of Saturday's game would get to attend the Leadership for Educators conference in NYC in the fall. Normally teacher conferences were in the category of "a necessary evil," but this was *the* conference. The number was capped at a couple hundred, so tickets were hard to come by. And instead of a middling hotel in the middle of nowhere, this was at a fancy hotel in Midtown Manhattan.

An all-expenses-paid three-day weekend in the city at a conference she could actually learn something from?

Crap. She was going to have to learn a little something about softball.

Luckily, she knew just the guy to help her.

Not so luckily, she may or may not have thrown a baseball through the kitchen window of his rental house yesterday.

Whoops.

Carter had been good-natured about it, but unsurprisingly, he hadn't exactly dashed to schedule their next baseball session, which meant . . .

Olive went to the window and used two fingers to peek between her mini-blinds to make sure Carter's truck was in the driveway. She had a little groveling to do.

Olive was already on her front porch when she halted, realizing it was barely seven in the morning, and that if she were going to ask the guy a favor, the least she could do was brush her teeth. And maybe do something about her tired purple bathrobe and frog slippers. Olive found them to be comfy and charming, but Carter was no doubt more accustomed to seeing women in silk and stockings. She owned neither, but by God, she could and would at least brush her hair.

Olive trudged upstairs and stuck her toothbrush in her mouth as she surveyed her closet, wishing she had one of those baseball-style tees with the colored sleeves. Maybe if she looked the part of a baseball player, he'd be more likely to take another chance on her.

Instead, she settled for her favorite workout outfit—a hot pink sports bra, black muscle tank, and short shorts that she thought did nice things to show off her toned legs. Carter had said once that he liked her legs, and a woman with Olive's distinct lack of typical feminine charm had to leverage her assets however she could.

She drew the line at wearing makeup, though she did wash her face and pull her hair into an intentionally messy bun. She practiced a smile in the mirror, the sort of demure smile that she imagined made Felicity look freaking *darling*.

Olive, on the other hand, looked constipated.

She sighed and decided Carter was either going to help her or he wouldn't. Feminine wiles would have nothing to do with it.

Olive pulled on her bright orange gym shoes, which complemented her outfit not in the least but made her happy, and trotted said shoes across both of their freshly mowed lawns, thanks to Carter, and up the steps to his front door.

She knocked only once, the barest nod toward politeness before trying the door handle, since they'd sort of skipped the *get to know each other* phase of being neighbors and gone straight to space invasion. At least as far as Olive was concerned.

The faint smell of coffee hit her nostrils—coffee that, if she wasn't mistaken, was more expensive and more delicious than hers. She followed the scent.

"Carter?" she called, walking into his kitchen. She didn't find the man, but she did find a coffeepot and, lifting the silver carafe, discovered it full. "Too much for one person," she said aloud to the empty room. "I'll help you with this."

She pulled down a boring white mug—the kind people put into rental homes—from the cupboard and poured herself a cup, then helped herself to a splash of milk from his fridge. Olive took a sip and gave a slow sigh of pleasure. As expected, his coffee was better than hers.

Olive glanced at the duct tape and plastic currently covering the broken window, and winced. She'd called Kenny Leaverson, Haven's go-to glass guy, on Carter's behalf after the incident yesterday, but he wasn't able to make it out until this afternoon.

On second thought, maybe she should ask her favor away from the scene of the crime.

"Yo. Carter," she called again, wandering into the hallway, mug still in hand. "Where did you get this magic coffee? And will I have to cash out my 403(b) to be able to afford some?"

The only response was a faint crashing sound from upstairs. She lifted her eyebrows. The thud wasn't quite big enough to be panic inducing, but it was definitely the sound of someone having a bad morning.

"Carter?" She rested one hand on the banister, hesitating for only a second.

Who was she kidding? She'd been dying to see upstairs since he'd moved in.

"I'm coming up," she said, making her way up the carpeted staircase. "If you've got lady company, now's the time for her to throw on one of your shirts that will no doubt inexplicably dwarf her, making her look all flustered and delicate."

"Go away," came the sharp bark.

She smiled. Ooh! Grumpy Carter was the *best*.

Olive followed the sound of the irritable command into the bedroom at the end of the hall, taking in the unmade king bed with a floral bedspread that there was no chance he'd picked out himself.

No sign of Carter.

She heard a muffled oath, followed it into the adjoining master bathroom, and stopped short. "Oh my."

A can of shave cream was on the tiled floor, likely the source of the crash she'd heard, but that wasn't the cause of her exclamation. Her *oh my* was inspired by a much more worthy cause: Carter Ramsey shirtless.

Correction: Carter Ramsey shirtless and angry.

Without the navy towel knotted at his waist, it'd be Carter Ramsey naked and angry.

"Did you not hear the 'go away'?" he asked, giving her the briefest of glances in the mirror.

She ignored this and set her coffee mug on the counter. "You need some help?"

"No," he snapped.

She ignored this, too, as she stepped closer, because the man obviously needed another hand. Two of them. And hers were the only ones nearby, so he didn't exactly have a lot of options.

Carter turned toward her, probably to roar at her to get out of his bathroom, but she reached out and, taking both his shoulders in her hands, turned him the other way so she could see his back.

"What the hell did you do here?" she asked in bemusement, taking in the tangled-up sling, which was bunched, twisted, and pulled uncomfortably taut against his shoulder blades. Instead of creating a comfortable rest for his injured arm, the sling now pinned his cast awkwardly against his chest.

"I hate this thing," he muttered under his breath.

"Can't say that I blame you," she said, reaching out and experimentally pulling on the twisted material.

Her fingertips brushed the skin of his back, and he went completely still, glancing over to meet her gaze in the mirror.

They stared at each other in the glass for a long moment, and her mouth was almost entirely dry as she forced herself to swallow, the sound audible in the steamy bathroom.

His skin was still warm from his shower, and just slightly damp, either from the shower as well, or from sweat—he looked to have been wrestling with this thing for a while—and she was suddenly aware of how . . . intimate the moment was.

And how very wifely, or at least girlfriendy, her presumption to help him had been.

"I thought you were supposed to be coordinated," she said, trying to find their usual banter-filled equilibrium.

"It's a pain in the ass to put on myself," he said with a sigh. "And when my skin's wet, it becomes downright impossible."

"Why didn't you wait for your skin to dry?" she asked, tugging at the sling again, trying to find a way to create some slack.

"Well damn, Olive. Brilliant idea. Really useful *hindsight* advice in my current predicament. Quick, get the time machine!"

"Sarcasm's not going to detangle you."

"Neither are you, apparently. What are you doing back there?"

She plucked at a particularly taut part of the strap and let it snap back against his skin sharply. "Do you want help or not?"

"Is that what you call this? Help?"

"Impossible man," she muttered. "I'm just going to have to unfasten the whole thing. Where's the buckle?"

"Cutting into my jugular and strangling me," he groused. "But it's all slick from my shaving cream, and the damn thing slips every time I try to unbuckle it."

Carter turned around to face her.

Olive blinked. And stared. If seeing his naked back had been intimate, coming face-to-face with his bare chest added a borderline erotic charge to the moment. He seemed to feel it, too, because for once, neither had a single smart-ass comment.

Olive cleared her throat. "I'll just . . ." Her hands reached tentatively toward the buckle, which was indeed inexplicably pressed against his throat. Her hands hesitated for a moment, before reaching out once more. "I'll just see if I can unbuckle this."

She carefully avoided his eyes as her fingers worked to first flatten the twisted strap; then using two hands because the damn thing was slippery, she squeezed both ends of the buckle until it released with a quiet *snap*.

Carter exhaled in relief, his breath minty fresh against her face, and before she could rethink the wisdom of it, Olive lifted her gaze to his.

If her breath had hitched before, now it straight up caught in her throat, and she felt a little light-headed at his nearness. For the first time, she fully understood the big deal about Carter Ramsey. He was always attractive, objectively, but up close, with no one around, there was a magnetism about him that even she, practical, implacable Olive Dunn, couldn't deny. There was a strength about him that she wanted to lean on, a kindness about him that she wanted to cling to, and a raw masculinity that had her fingers itching to reach for the knot of the towel at his waist.

"Thank you," he murmured, and for a horrible second, Olive wondered if she'd said it all aloud, and he was thanking her for the gross amount of flattering thoughts she'd just had. Then he reached up, tugging the loosened sling from around his neck and pulling it free of his torso, and she realized he'd just been referring to her help with his sling.

"Shouldn't you put on a shirt before the sling?" she asked curiously.

"I was hot," he muttered. "I'm allowed to walk around shirtless in my own home in summer."

"Sure, sure. Benefit of being a guy, I suppose," Olive said distractedly, peering more closely at the tattoo on his left arm that she was seeing fully for the first time. She'd assumed that when she saw the entire thing up close, she'd know what it was, but it just looked like an abstract pattern.

"What am I looking at here?" she asked, reaching out and tracing a finger along one of the lines, starting at his shoulder and ending just above his elbow.

Carter stilled and made a sort of hissing noise that had her snatching her hand back.

"Sorry. Is it . . . sensitive?"

"Yes, though not in the way you think," he said, irritably. "And the ink's just that—ink."

"But why'd you choose it?"

"I didn't," he said with a sheepish smile. "I was twenty-one, all the other guys on the team were doing it, but unlike them, I didn't have a motivational quote, or cross, or girl's name I wanted commemorated forever, so I just picked a random pattern from the binder and went with it."

"What about Felicity's name?" she asked, unable to stop herself. "Did you consider that?"

Carter's gaze locked on hers and held for a long moment. "No. I did not."

Olive felt an uncomfortable sense of relief, and instead focused on the tattoo, though without touching this time. "It's weirdly sort of . . . hot."

"Why *weirdly?*"

She shrugged. "Honestly? If you would have asked me five minutes ago, I'd have said I don't really get tattoos. But I can see how some lady-folk would see otherwise."

"Some ladyfolk," he said with a small smile. "But not you?"

She tapped her temple. "Too smart to fall for the likes of you."

Too aware that you'd break my heart.

"Ah," Carter said softly.

For a long moment they stood in the humid bathroom, though strangely the steam seemed to be coming more from *them* than the aftermath of his shower.

Finally Carter gave a quick shake of his head.

"What are you doing here, anyway?" he asked, tossing the sling onto the counter and extending the elbow of his injured arm gently, but repeatedly, stretching the joint.

"Oh, I—" Why had she come over here, again? His near nakedness made it hard to think.

"That's my mug. Are you drinking my coffee?" he asked, nodding toward the mug. Before she could answer, he picked it up and took a long swallow. Then another. "Yup," he answered the question for himself.

"It's really good," she said. "Like *really* good."

He grinned. "I know. I like nice things and can afford them."

Olive rolled her eyes, a quick response on the tip of her tongue until she realized she was still standing unnecessarily close to him.

She was about to step back in embarrassment when it dawned on her that *he* hadn't moved away, either. Now that he was free of the tangled sling, there was no reason for them to be standing in the cramped bathroom, much less face-to-face with only a few inches between them, and yet neither had made any effort to move away.

Granted, he had less room to move than she did, with only the toilet and shower behind him, but he could have, if he wanted to. And he didn't.

The realization was . . . intriguing.

"So?" he said, leaning his hip against the counter as he took another sip of coffee, and continued to look down at her.

"So, what?"

His eyebrows lifted as he gestured in a wide circle with the coffee mug. "What are you doing in my house—uninvited?"

"Saving your ass, apparently," she said, reaching up and snagging the coffee mug, taking a sip of her own. "And you're welcome."

"Only you would think you're due a thank-you for breaking and entering."

"I'll confess to the entering, but I didn't break a damn thing. Your door was unlocked."

"Because the other day, when I didn't leave it unlocked, you rattled the door for ten minutes."

"Because you were ignoring me," she said pragmatically.

"Because I was on the bike, with headphones, and didn't hear you."

"Which is exactly why you should leave your door unlocked," Olive pointed out.

Carter inhaled, then let it out slowly. "You exhaust me."

She held up the coffee mug as she stepped backward. "I pair nicely with caffeine. I'm going to go refill this, pour you a cup of your own, and then we can get to discussing how you can repay me for my nursing duties," she said, pointing at the discarded sling.

"Here's a counteroffer," he said. "Pour me a cup of my own without the milk, complete said nursing duties by helping me put the sling on correctly, and you can explain what was so urgent that you had to break into my house."

"Fair enough," she agreed; then her eyes widened with panic when he picked up the sling and held it out to her. "Not here. Bring it downstairs after you're dressed."

His smile was slow and gloating. "I knew it."

"You know nothing." Then she looked at him suspiciously. "Out of curiosity, what do you think you know?"

He leaned forward, closing the distance between them once more. "That you're very aware of what's under this towel."

Olive refused to let her gaze drift downward, but oh, how she wanted it to. "What's that? More misplaced ego?"

His smile grew. "Nothing misplaced about it."

"Calm yourself," she said, boldly stepping toward him and giving him a deliberately disinterested pat on the cheek. "Because I know something, too."

"What do you think you know?" he said, echoing her question as she turned away.

Olive turned back and flashed a confident smile over her shoulder as she paused in the doorway. "That whatever's under that towel is very aware of me, too."

Chapter Fifteen

Thursday, August 20

Carter let out a reluctant laugh as Olive charged out of the bathroom to go help herself to more of his coffee. Just when he thought he had a fighting chance of getting the upper hand with the woman, she rose to the challenge and knocked his ego right back down to size.

Though she hadn't been wrong. The mental and emotional aspect of his manhood might be kept firmly in check when Olive was around. The physical proof, though . . .

He glanced down.

No doubt about it. Physically, he'd been fully, uncomfortably aware of Olive Dunn.

He dragged a hand over his face, trying to sort through just what he thought about that. It's not as though her nearness had been sexually motivated. Her touch hadn't been meant to seduce. She'd merely been helping out an invalid who embarrassingly still hadn't gotten the hang of the damn sling.

But it hadn't mattered. He'd been sexually aware and seduced all the same.

Hell. He'd probably have kissed her had she not moved away when she had. He'd have sunk his fingers into that thick hair and kissed all that tart sass right off her lips until he tasted the sweetness that he was increasingly certain might be lurking beneath the good-ol'-Olive routine. Had the sense that it would take only the tug for her to collide against him, send that friend-zone wall they'd built tumbling to the ground, and the results would be . . .

Explosive.

Carter blew out a breath and shook his head, wondering if he needed a cold shower before heading downstairs. Instead, he settled for splashing cold water on his face.

Going into the bedroom, he tugged on jeans, then pulled a white button-down shirt out of the closet. He'd have preferred a T-shirt, but he'd learned the hard way that those were obnoxious to get on and off given his injury. He shoved his casted arm through one of the sleeves, slid on the other, and left the buttons undone. Not to see if Olive would check out his chest again, but because buttoning the damn things with the fingers of his left hand largely immobilized was a pain.

But yeah, okay. A little to see if Olive would check out his pecs again.

He was disappointed.

When he walked into the kitchen, she barely looked up from the newspaper she'd helped herself to.

"You get the *Wall Street Journal* and the *New York Times*?" she asked, taking a sip of her coffee as she turned the page of the *WSJ*. "Fancy. Do you actually read them?"

"I like the pictures."

"Aha!" she said, hearing his true meaning beneath the sarcasm as she did every time. "So you *do* read them. It can't be easy with as much as you travel and train."

"It's not," he acknowledged, accepting the coffee she slid across the counter with a nod of thanks. "But it's actually because I'm busy that I started the habit a few years ago. Life of a pro can be . . . isolating. You're surrounded largely by people in your sport, and even when you have time away from your teammates, coaches, agent, whatever, you can't go anywhere without being surrounded by a swarm of fans. If you're not careful, you'll forget there's a whole world outside of baseball."

Olive heaved out a huge sigh.

He frowned. "What?"

"It's so annoying," she said, folding the newspaper closed.

"What is?" Carter took a sip of coffee. It *was* excellent.

"All your hidden depths."

"Starting to fall for me now, are you?"

"Let's not get crazy."

"And yet, you're here in my home, checking me out naked in my bathroom," he reminded her. "Still waiting on an explanation for that, by the way."

"First things first," she said, leaning across the counter and grabbing the sling he'd brought downstairs with him. She palmed it. "This one's dry."

"I've got a few spare straitjackets."

"Get tangled in them often?" she asked, coming around the counter.

"More often than I'd like."

"You have like a billion dollars. You could hire some cute little nurse to hang around the house and help you," she pointed out.

I'd rather have you.

He bit the insane thought back before it slipped out, though the notion seemed even more plausible with the competent way she looped the strap around his neck. Gently, but firmly, she positioned his arm at a right angle in the sling and then clipped it into place.

"There we go," she murmured, straightening out a part of the strap at his collarbone that had folded under. Her tone and touch were almost tender, and his heart skipped a little at seeing this new side of her. He wanted more of it. More of her.

"Olive." Before he could think better of it, his hand lifted, closing over hers.

She froze, her eyes, wide with panic, flying to his before she jerked her hand away and stepped back. "I have a favor."

"Okay," he said slowly, forcing his brain to shift gears from disappointment to hearing her out.

"But first, do you have that time machine for real?"

"Why?" Carter asked warily.

"Because hypothetically, if I could undo that . . ." She jerked her thumb toward his broken window.

"Your aim really is impossibly bad," he said, smiling a little to show he was joking.

"It isn't that bad."

"You threw the ball *behind* you instead of toward me. I barely knew that was possible."

"You see!" she wailed. "That's why I'm here. I need your help!"

"I'm not sure even my skills are up to that."

"Don't lose your cocky edge now. The teacher softball game is on Saturday, and I need to not be horrible."

"You're planning on going now? I thought you were going to claim you had distemper. Which, by the way, I googled, and it's a dog disease."

"Exactly. Nobody will have heard of it, so they'll assume it's very real, very serious, and they won't mind that I'm not playing. But that's old news. Now I need to not only play, I need to be *exceptional*."

He lifted his eyebrows.

"Oh, come on," she pleaded. "If anyone can turn me into a superstar in forty-eight hours, it's you."

"Flattery is a weird look on you. What changed?"

"I found out what Principal Mullins's bribe is."

"If it's a new kitchen window, I wanna play," Carter said.

"Don't be a baby, it's summer. The plastic works fine."

"A bee got in here this morning."

Olive's eyes went wide. "Not a *bee*! I hope it doesn't come next door, I haven't built my bomb shelter yet."

"How do you know I'm not allergic?" Carter pointed out.

"Because we went to grade school together, and the faculty always used to make a point of Jill Wheeler being allergic to bee stings. Carter Ramsey? Not so much."

"Your memory creeps me out," Carter muttered. "Okay, so what's your boss's bribe that's so compelling?"

"Whoever he names MVP at the game on Saturday gets to go to this super fancy teacher conference. Not the bad kind with watery coffee in an off-the-freeway hotel that smells like weird cheese, but in a nice hotel in the city with cappuccino machines and fancy croissants, and the entire lobby smells like patchouli."

Carter rubbed his temple. The woman really could be exhausting.

"So?" she said impatiently.

"A teacher conference? Really? That's what I'm risking my windows for?"

"Please." Her plea was undercut by the stomping of her foot, but was cute all the same. "It's in the city, and I never get to go to Manhattan, much less expenses paid!"

Carter had been about to pour more coffee, but his attention snapped to her. "You're coming to Manhattan?"

"If I'm MVP, yes," she said, still impatient.

Carter grinned. "*I* live in New York City. Will I see you? When's the conference?"

She blinked, looking so genuinely stunned by the question that his chest felt tight for a moment. "October. Do you *want* to see me?"

Very much.

The strength of the longing was startling, and discomfiting. As was the fact that he wanted desperately to ask if *she* wanted to see *him* again after he left Haven in a few weeks.

Carter shoved away the urge and took a large, bracing swallow of coffee. At no point had he planned *not* to help her. But now he had some skin in the game, too—the chance to see Olive again after their time here together was over.

"All right," he said. "If we've only got two days to turn you into a ballplayer, we'd better get started."

Olive lit up in a way that made *him* light up. "Right now?"

"Let me make a few phone calls," Carter replied. "See if I can find us a space to keep you away from all things breakable."

"You get me. You *so* get me," she said, topping off both their coffee mugs.

He *did* get Olive. More than he'd ever gotten anyone. Just like she got him. Now, if only he knew what to do about it.

Chapter Sixteen

Thursday, August 20

"I'm *really* terrible," Olive said, panting a little as she pushed the helmet back and blinked up at him, her cheeks shiny with sweat. "Worse than I thought."

Carter lifted his cap and used his forearm to wipe his own damp forehead from the ninety-degree August heat. It had taken him longer than expected to figure out their practice situation, and by the time they'd gotten to the field, the day was already in peak heat.

Her shoulders slumped at his silence, and he gently pounded a fist against the top of her helmet. "Hey. You're not that bad."

She *was* that bad. Olive didn't just miss every ball she swung at; she missed it by a solid foot. And they hadn't gotten to fielding yet, but judging from the way she missed him by a mile every time she tossed the ball back to the pitcher's mound, he didn't have high hopes for that, either.

So yes, she was truly terrible at baseball. But Carter was truly excellent at it. And he had no intention of letting his protégé get anywhere near the field on Saturday until she at least had a shot of making contact with the ball.

"We've only been at it for an hour or so," he said gently. "Now get some water, fix your ponytail, and get back in there."

"What's wrong with my ponytail?" she said as she retrieved her water bottle and took several healthy gulps.

"Well, for starters, it quit being a ponytail," he said, picking up her hair band from the dirt.

"Oh." She took another gulp of water, then took the hair band from him and pulled off her helmet, shoving it at his chest. "Do I seriously have to wear that thing?"

"The helmet? Yes. Safety first, Dunn. As a teacher, you should know that."

"Yeah, yeah, yeah, but this isn't a classroom full of sixteen-year-olds with scalpels and dead frogs, nor is it Yankee Stadium. And your throws are going nowhere near my head."

"True. But I'm going to go out on a limb here and say whoever's pitching on Saturday won't be as good as me."

"You're a pitcher?" she asked, flipping her hair over, Cousin It style, and pulling it into a high knot atop her head.

He gaped at her, too distracted by how little she knew about his career to even be allured by the way her hair curled at the nape of her neck, or even by the thought of how if he kissed that spot right now, it'd probably be just slightly salty, and he'd have to go in for another . . .

He shook his head in disbelief. "You don't even know what position I play?"

She flipped her head back up and gave him a huge grin. *Gotcha.*

"Aren't you just so amusing," he said, replacing his cap and backing toward the mound. "As punishment, break time is over."

Olive groaned, but put the helmet back on her head, giving it a smack with her palm to flatten it over the knot of her hair. Even without the long blonde hair peeking from beneath the blue helmet he'd borrowed from the JV baseball coach, there was zero chance of her being mistaken for a boy. The long tan legs in short jean shorts were undeniably feminine, and the way she filled out her plain white tee was definitely all woman.

Distracted, his next pitch went well wide of the plate, but she swung at it anyway and missed by a mile. She ran to retrieve the ball and tossed it back to him. This time he only had to lean off the mound rather than leave it altogether to catch the ball. *Progress.*

"How was I supposed to hit that?" she asked, resuming her place behind the plate.

"You weren't. Remember that whole ball-versus-strike thing I explained? That was a ball."

"I'm beginning to think all career accolades you've racked up over the years are a scam," she said, waggling her bat over her shoulder with far more confidence than was warranted, but then this *was* Olive.

But Carter was no stranger to confidence himself. His next pitch was overhand, a fastball that she had no hope of hitting.

"Couldn't you have just flexed your muscles?" she grumbled, chasing after the ball.

His point made, Carter's next pitch was a slow underhand, also right over the plate, and for the first time, she made contact.

Olive let out a delighted noise. "I hit it!"

"You sure as hell did," he said, not having the heart to explain that it had barely glanced her bat and would have been a foul ball. From his place on the mound, he gave her an air high five and laughed in surprise when she did the exact same thing, at the exact same time.

Thank God his teammates couldn't see him, laughing on the same field of his high school days, playing with a woman who closed her eyes eight out of ten times she swung at the ball. And having the time of his life.

"You know what you did differently that time?" Carter called as he dived to his left to catch her errant toss.

She heaved out a sigh and adjusted her helmet. "You're not going to tell me something inane like 'I kept my eye on the ball,' are you?"

Carter stuck his tongue in his cheek as he walked toward home plate, because that had been exactly what he was going to say. "Okay, let's try something new," he said.

She planted a hand on her hip and gave him a mutinous look. "If you think I'm going to fall for that ploy where the guy teaches the girl how to play sports by pressing up against her back in a doggy-style position, I'll warn you now—I won't."

With a defeated laugh, he dropped his head forward, burying his face in his hand, trying to decide if he was amused, horrified, or aroused.

When Carter lifted his head, Olive was still giving him a suspicious look.

"That is not what I was going to suggest," he assured her, though he couldn't help but think the idea held increasing appeal when she cocked her hip to the side like that, calling attention to the impressive curves of her lower body.

He had no doubt if he ever got his hands on her, she'd be an intoxicating combination of slim and full, firm and soft . . .

Carter cleared his throat. "Your swing is fine. That isn't your problem."

"*Fine*. High praise, Coach."

"Be quiet. Get back in position."

She gave him a mocking salute, but did as he said.

"Okay, this time when I toss the ball," he explained, "don't worry about hitting it. You can swing, or not swing, but your only mission is to watch the ball the entire time it comes over the plate, okay? Don't worry about anything else other than staring at the ball the entire time it crosses the plate. Pretend the ball is someone who just told you that science is stupid, and then burn it with the heat of your death gaze."

"So this *is* a *keep your eye on the ball* thing."

"Well, aren't you just sharp as a tack. Now shut up and do what I say."

She shrugged and got in position. Carter underhanded the ball, extra careful to make sure this one sailed right down the center of the plate, where she . . . hit it.

Carter was more accustomed to the sound of a sharp *crack* of a wooden bat on a baseball. But the softer *thunk* of an aluminum bat against a softball was pretty damn gratifying as well. Even more gratifying was Olive's huge grin as he deliberately let it sail over his shoulder into the outfield instead of making the semieasy catch.

"I did it! I did it!" She raised her arms over her head in victory with a whoop, then dropped them again, sticking the bat between her legs and riding it around like some sort of ridiculous horse while her other arm made a lassoing motion, whooping the entire time.

He smiled as he watched her, shaking his head. "You know you're supposed to run to first base, right?"

"Don't ruin a good thing with running," she called back, still doing her awkward victory dance. "Don't they do this in football after a touchdown?"

"I don't think anyone does whatever that is," he said, walking toward her. "Now, on Saturday, you have to promise me you'll run to first base when you hit the ball."

"Sure, whatever," she said, her smile still reaching from ear to ear. "I. Hit. The. Ball." She poked a finger into his stomach with each word. "Did you see?"

"Yeah, yeah. I saw."

She poked her finger again into his side, and he grimaced, moving away. Olive narrowed her eyes. "Did that hurt?"

"Of course not. It just . . . Stop it."

Her eyes went wide. "Oh my God. You're ticklish! Carter Ramsey's six-pack is ticklish!"

She reached out again, this time in a deliberate tickling motion, and he let out a laugh as he batted her hand away. "Knock it off."

But she had two hands, and he had only one good one, and she took full advantage, diving at him with both hands, as he squirmed to get away from her searching fingers. "This is no way to repay me for my help," he said with a helpless laugh as he tried and failed to get away from her.

His stomach had been ticklish for as long as he could remember, but for obvious reasons, he let few people know it. Giggling wasn't exactly part of his brand.

"This is the best," Olive said, sneaking a finger behind the elbow of his injured arm and tickling as he let out another involuntary laugh.

"Stop!" he laughed helplessly.

She didn't. Realizing he couldn't get away from her, short of running away from her and having her chase him around the baseball field, Carter came up with the only other solution he could think of.

Waiting until her questing fingers moved to his front once again, he wrapped his good arm around Olive and jerked her against him, pinning her arms between them, rendering her fingers mostly immobile.

"Hey!" she cried in protest against his chest, her voice muffled.

"You are not the aggrieved party here," Carter replied, catching his breath.

"Okay, I'll stop," she said.

"Uh-huh."

He didn't know that he believed her, but that was not why he didn't release her. He didn't release her because he really didn't want to. Olive's warm, sturdy body against his felt better than it had any right to. Better than any daydream, and there'd been a few lately.

But as nice as it was, it was torture, too, having her pressed against him chest to chest, hip to hip, without being able to touch her. Since he couldn't use his hands, he settled for relishing the softness of full breasts against his chest, the sweet and slightly spicy scent of her that he suddenly couldn't get enough of. The sheer *warmth* of her, her body and her soul.

He dipped his head slightly, then laughed when his jaw brushed the hard helmet she still wore. How was it possible that the sexiest moment of his life was somehow also the unsexiest?

"Carter?" she asked quietly. Her voice was questioning, but she didn't move away, and he pulled back enough to look down at her, just as her face lifted to his. "I won't tickle you anymore," she said softly.

He nodded, but his gaze was on her mouth. He'd forgotten all about the tickling. Forgotten all about her first hit. Forgotten the reason they were here in the first place.

In fact, he couldn't even think about anything other than what she would do if he lowered his face and brushed his lips over hers.

His head dipped slightly, and her lips parted in surprise. But she didn't move away, and Carter felt a thrill of victory that rivaled anything he'd ever felt on the baseball field as his mouth lowered—

"Yo! Ramsey!"

He wasn't sure who jerked back faster at the interruption. But even after they'd put several inches between them, Carter's and Olive's gazes stayed locked a crucial moment longer before they both turned toward the sound of the voice.

"Sorry we're late," Jakey said, jogging up the grass hill from the parking lot, glove and bat tucked under his arm. "Took me forever to get the troops into my minivan."

"Yeah, but your troops aren't the ones who made us stop for doughnuts," said a woman emerging over the crest of the hill as well, armed with a box of pink doughnuts. She grinned at them. "Hey, Carter. Hey, Olive."

"Kelly!" Olive said in surprise when she saw Kelly Blakely. "What are you doing here?"

"I called them," Carter said, glancing down at her. "Well, texted."

"For what?"

"News flash, babe," Jakey said, wrapping an arm around Olive's neck when he was close enough. "Baseball's a team sport. Can't be learned with two people, even if one of them is a semidecent player," he said with a grin at Carter.

"Kelly," called another male voice. "Question. Where are the bats? When I told you to 'grab the stuff,' what did you think I meant?"

The pretty blonde held up the pink box and looked quizzically over at her husband, who joined them. "Doughnuts. Obviously. Carter Ramsey, you're even better looking in person. Doughnut?"

Mark Blakely rolled his eyes and deposited a couple of helmets to the ground, then came over to shake Carter's hand. "Good to see you, man. Sorry I haven't been able to before now. I've been back and forth to the city."

Carter didn't know Mark all that well, and he didn't know Kelly at all, but Jakey had said they were friends with Olive and would be down for playing a quick game of softball.

"Mark's opening up another restaurant," Kelly said proudly, winding her arm around her husband's waist. "This one's in Midtown, right in the middle of all the swanky office buildings, where the corporate credit cards mean cha-ching!"

"Very classy, babe," Mark said, smiling as he pressed a kiss against the side of her head.

"What? I teach kindergarten," Kelly said. "One of us has to make bank, and it's not going to be me. Olive understands."

"Me?" Olive said. "Nope. I like getting paid next to nothing, working ten-hour days to grade papers and create lesson plans, while spending my own money to supplement lab supplies because my boss thinks high school science isn't 'real world' stuff."

Olive and Kelly exchanged a look of teacher commiseration, and Carter felt a surge of frustration on their behalf as well as a flicker of guilt.

Yes, he had worked damn hard to get where he was. He'd been waking up every morning at four a.m. to train as long as he could remember. He put in five miles every damned day before heading to the gym, and that was in addition to the hours of scheduled practice time. When he wasn't keeping his body in peak condition, he exercised his mind, studying gameplay constantly, both his own and his opponents. Not to mention the PR obligations. The interviews, the photo shoots, the advertisements for his sponsors. Carter's life hardly mirrored the whisky-swilling, model-dating image the paparazzi captured on a rare night off.

But he also knew people like Kelly and Olive worked just as hard to make in a year what he made in a single day. And it didn't feel right.

"Be right back," Mark said, jogging back to the car, presumably to get the bats Kelly had forgotten.

"You guys are seriously here to help me?" Olive asked, looking around. "I'm not sure Carter spelled out just how hopeless a case I am."

"Oh, I let them know," he told her with a wink.

She rolled her eyes, but grinned.

Out of the corner of his eye, he saw Kelly's eyebrows lift, but he ignored her. It wasn't as though he had any answers as to what the hell was going on with him and Olive. Not even for himself.

"All right, Kelly, I'm putting you on first. Mark, how's your pitching?" Carter asked the other man, who'd just rejoined them.

"Passable."

"Good, you're on the mound. Jakey, I need you behind the plate. Easy grounders toward left field."

"You got it," Jakey said, slinging his bat over his shoulder as Kelly and Mark grabbed mitts, squabbling over whether the shape of the clouds predicted which movie they should watch tonight (Kelly was convinced a stiletto-shaped cloud indicated *Sex and the City* was in their future), or whether it was just a function of standard weather patterns (Mark's stance: a cloud was a cloud).

"Where should I go?" Olive asked.

"Hold on," he said, jogging over to the bench where he'd dropped his stuff when they'd arrived an hour earlier. When Carter jogged back, he placed a baseball cap on her head that matched his own, only smaller. One he'd had his assistant overnight him.

She lifted it and looked at the front, then laughed. "Figures. You're trying to turn me into a Hawks fan."

"Wrong. I'm trying to turn you into a Carter Ramsey fan."

"Unfortunately, I think I already am," she grumbled under her breath.

He leaned down until his face was just a few inches from hers, grinning. "What was that?"

"I said I hate you?" She smiled back as she pulled her hair out of its topknot and into a low ponytail, then replaced the cap.

"It looks good on you," he said, flicking a finger over the bill. "You're one of my fangirls now."

"You're highly disturbed. I'm getting worried."

"Hey, guys, we playing or what?" Jakey called.

"Yup," Carter called back, handing Olive a glove, and motioning for her to follow him. "Come on, Dunn. Time to brush up your glove skills in the best position there is."

"Repose?" she said, reluctantly following after him.

"Shortstop," he replied, pointing between second and third base. "Stand there."

"What will you do?" she asked, taking his usual position.

"Hover around third. Bark orders and criticism as the ball comes your way over and over," he replied.

"Can I have that job?"

"Let's see how this first hit goes, then we'll talk."

Jakey's first grounder shot straight between her feet and into the outfield.

She gave him a droll look. "I suppose I could use a little practice."

Carter lifted his casted arm as best he could to pinch his thumb and forefinger together with a sliver of space between them. *Just a little*.

"Olive! Babe!" Kelly called. "You have to go get the ball." She punched her own glove with her fist. "Throw it here for practice."

Olive did as instructed. Her arm was good. Her aim, on the other hand, sent the ball sailing between first and second base, a good six feet wide of Kelly, who had to go darting into right field to retrieve it.

Which sent Olive running after her to apologize. Then, with the ball lying in the grass between them, they began chatting.

Jakey shook his head at home plate and pulled his phone out of his back pocket to kill time until the ball made it back his way.

Mark crossed his arms on the pitcher's mound, watching the women chatting in the outfield a moment before glancing over at Carter. "You realize you owe us for this, right?"

Carter sighed, even as he motioned for Olive to get her ass back to the correct side of the field. "I know."

"I'm thinking wings and beers after this. On you," Mark said with a smile.

"Wings and *whisky* after this," Jakey corrected, not looking up from his phone. "Really expensive whisky."

"Done," Carter said amicably, not minding in the least, even though technically, it was Olive they were all doing the favor for, not Carter. He'd just been the one to ask on her behalf.

Plus, whisky and wings with friends after a casual game of ball sounded damn nice. It sounded like the kind of thing he could get used to.

And, he thought, as a grinning Olive trotted back to him, exactly the kind of thing he shouldn't get used to.

Chapter Seventeen

Saturday, August 22

"I owe you an apology," Olive said, lifting the hem of her green Haven High T-shirt to wipe the sweat from her face. "This baseball thing is really hard."

"Well, to be fair," Carter said, propping one foot up on the bench beside her and popping a pistachio in his mouth, "you've been making it way harder than it should be. I've never seen a third baseman—woman—run quite so much."

She took a swig of water and glared up at him. "The damn thing just keeps going between my legs."

He popped another pistachio in his mouth and grinned down at her.

"Yeah, yeah. I heard it," she grumbled.

The game had been paused for the past ten minutes or so due to a possible sprained ankle on the other team, and Carter had jogged over to keep her company during the break.

"At least the entire town didn't show up," Carter said sarcastically, gesturing to the completely full stands behind her. "Damn," he swore irritably at a pistachio he couldn't crack. "These things are easier to eat with two good hands."

Distractedly, Olive pulled the pistachio out of his fingers and opened it, reaching up to shove the nut into his mouth herself. "The crowd is your fault, you know. Nobody would have bothered to come see the high school staff play softball in ninety-degree weather if *the* Carter Ramsey hadn't agreed to be the referee. And your magazine hasn't even hit the stands yet. What happens then, it turns into a full circus?"

"Guess we'll find out soon," he grumbled, though he didn't look quite as haunted at the mention of the *Citizen* magazine feature anymore. She wondered if he was coming to grips with the fact that he deserved that Man of the Year honor, even if he did have only one good arm at the moment.

"And it's ump," he said, chewing the pistachio.

"Huh?" she said, not following.

"It's called an umpire in baseball. Not referee."

"Oh yeah?" she said sweetly. "I can think of another name for it."

"Why are you mad at me?" he said. "I've made nothing but fair calls."

"I've struck out. Twice."

"Swinging," he pointed out. "That's not on me."

"Not helpful," she said testily, even as she lifted her hand to smile and wave at Mark and Kelly, who were sitting next to Carter's parents. "I'm never going to be the MVP at this rate."

Goodbye, teacher conference. Goodbye, seeing Carter in the city. Olive wasn't sure which one she was more bummed about. Or rather, she knew exactly which one she was more bummed about, and was trying hard to ignore it.

Instead she settled for glaring at him. "A little advice would not be unwelcome right now."

Carter shook his head. "The ump's a neutral third party. Wouldn't be fair."

She lifted a single threatening finger and looked pointedly at his ticklish torso.

Carter grunted as he fished another pistachio out of the bag. "Fine. *One* piece of advice, but you're not going to like it: you're taking your eye off the ball. Both at the plate and in the field."

She sighed. "How is such a simple concept so hard?"

"You'll get there," he said.

"Before the end of the game?" she asked. "There are only three more rounds."

"Innings. And actually, there are only two more. Nine innings in baseball, remember? Though it's a tie game, so it could go longer."

"Longer?" she asked, horrified.

Carter laughed. "Look, you've got one more at bat. Remember what we practiced. Think about nothing but staring at the ball all the way across the plate."

"I doubt it'll matter. Ginny Townsend's already hit two doubles. Why is a history teacher that good at softball?"

"Hey, look at that!" he said, tugging her ponytail. "You've quit calling them *duos.*"

She gave him a faint smile, but it didn't do much to improve her mood. This morning, she'd felt so ready for the game. After two straight days of practice with Carter, she was hardly going to quit her day job to become a softball player, but she'd been confident she could at least hit the freaking ball.

Misplaced confidence, apparently.

Olive tried to take solace in the fact that while she certainly wasn't the MVP, she also wasn't the worst on the team. The majority of her colleagues couldn't play softball for shit, either.

"Which one's Ginny Townsend?" Carter asked.

Olive gestured with her head, and he glanced over at the petite brunette talking with Principal Mullins.

"Ah yeah," he said. "She's obviously played before. But you've got an advantage."

She gazed at him skeptically. "If you're about to say something stupid like how I 'play with heart . . .'"

Carter reached out and gave her upper arm a squeeze. "You're stronger. If you can connect, you can hit the ball farther than anyone here, save perhaps that giant the other team's got playing first."

"Gary Russo. He's their gym teacher and football coach."

"Hey, Ump. Looks like we're back in business," Principal Mullins said, turning and hollering at Carter.

Her reprieve was over.

Carter lifted his hand in acknowledgment to Olive's boss, then looked back down at her. "Eye. Ball."

She made a crude gesture at his back as he returned to home plate.

"Felt that!" he called, without turning around.

Olive's team was up to bat, though she likely wouldn't be up until the next round, or inning, or whatever it was called, so she helped herself to Carter's pistachios, trying not to wince when Ginny got yet another hit. A single this time, but that made the history teacher three for three, and Olive zero for loser.

The next three at bats for Haven High were outs, which meant they ended the inning without scoring, and too soon, Olive was dragging herself out to third base, where she chatted with Rhinebeck's freshman English teacher, who had a bad back and was acting as third-base coach for her team.

Olive listened with half an ear as Sandra droned on about how parents "just weren't enforcing the importance of summer reading anymore," and her gaze and attention wandered to home plate, where Carter was chatting—flirting?—with a cute redhead teacher who was taking her sweet time stepping up to the plate.

Olive knew umpires usually wore the mask thingies, but either nobody had thought to bring one, or Carter had decided he didn't need it, because his face was on full display in all its annoyingly handsome Man of the Year glory.

No wonder it was a low-scoring softball game at 1–1. Most of the teachers were female, and Carter Ramsey was one hell of a distraction.

As though sensing her gaze on him, Carter's eyes flicked over to third base, and he gave her the quickest of winks before gesturing to the pitcher and hitter that it was time to get back to it.

Olive blew out an irritated breath, mostly at herself, because the damn wink made her feel warm and fluttery, as though there were something between them other than being neighbors and friends. As though he weren't waiting for the love of his life to return from California so they could make good on their idiotic pact and get married.

Carter hadn't brought up his and Felicity's arrangement again, and she was both grateful and disappointed. She wanted to know where his head was at. Wanted to know if, when Felicity showed up, everything would change.

The *clink* of the ball against a bat snapped her out of her reverie, just in time to see the softball rolling idly toward her. The redhead had evidently barely made contact, because the ball had all but come to a standstill by the time Olive got to it, scooping it out of the dirt and hurling it toward Penny Bell at first base, who, Olive was thrilled to note, only had to lean a little to her right to catch it.

"Safe!" Carter yelled from where he'd jogged down to first base.

"What?" Olive yelled back. "But I caught it! And threw it! And Penny caught the throw!"

"The batter beat your throw," he said, not looking at her as he jogged back to home plate.

Oh. Right. She'd sort of forgotten that was a part of it.

Still, Olive fumed through the rest of the inning, wishing for the first time all game that the ball would come her way, and angry, again, for the first time, when it didn't. She'd wanted a chance to show Carter what was what.

After the third out, she trotted back to the dugout, deliberately not looking at Carter as she did so. When she did sneak a look out of the corner of her eye after she switched her cap for one of the helmets, he was flirting again, this time with the pretty blonde catcher for the other team.

Maybe he should have worn the mask after all, because Olive wasn't entirely sure her bat wouldn't "slip" during her next at bat, which was coming up all too soon.

Principal Mullins was up first. He hit a solid single to right field.

The geometry teacher went next. A strikeout, which was just shocking, considering she'd spent the entire at bat giggling and flirting with the umpire. One out.

One of the two Haven PE teachers hit a double to left field, sending Principal Mullins to third.

The art teacher popped up. Two outs.

Olive's turn.

Crap.

She'd learned enough about the game over the past couple of weeks to know that in the final inning of a tie game, a runner on third base and two outs was a high-pressure situation. The excited cheering of the spectators in the bleachers confirmed it.

"You've got this!" Olive heard Kelly yell, followed by someone starting the chant, *bring him home, bring him home* . . .

Olive ordered herself not to look at Carter as she approached the plate, but the man was like a damn magnet for female eyes, and her gaze found him anyway.

He looked steadily back at her, and from the outside, there was nothing personal in the interaction. No words were exchanged, no flirty winks, not even a smile.

But somehow, she felt his support, knew that he was on her side. Not that he'd make a wrong call or throw the game in her favor, just that he was there. Win or lose.

"All right, let's do this," she said loudly, with a melodramatic sigh. "One more out, then it's barbecue time, am I right? That's the reason we're all here?"

The people near enough to hear laughed, and she stepped up to the plate, bat over her shoulder.

The first pitch sailed down the middle of the plate before she could even think to move.

"Strike!" Carter yelled.

She narrowed her eyes at him, and he shrugged.

The second ball also came sailing down the center of the plate—the Rhinebeck pitcher had played softball in college, and it showed. This time, Olive swung as hard as she could, nearly knocking herself over in the process. She was still regaining her balance when Carter yelled, "Strike," again.

"Yeah, yeah, we know," she snapped, unable to resist the urge to glare at him.

The ball had landed at his feet, and he picked it up before the catcher could, and he stared at it for a second too long before throwing it back to the pitcher.

Nobody else seemed to have noticed the moment, but Olive read the silent message loud and clear. *Keep your eye on the damn ball, Dunn.*

Fair enough. She was pretty sure she'd closed her eyes completely on that last one.

The ball came hurling her way once more and she practically burned a hole in it with her gaze—watching it carefully enough to know it was well wide of where it should be.

"Ball one," Carter yelled. He didn't look at her, but she swore she saw him give a single nod of approval.

The pitcher wound up again, and the process repeated. Once again, Olive concentrated on nothing but staring at that ball, only this time it was coming right down the center, and . . . she swung.

The sensation in her hands registered before the noise. A dull, delicious throb as the ball met the bat. Followed by a solid-sounding clanking noise.

Followed by what sounded like the entire bleachers yelling, *"Run!"*

She did. She sprinted toward first base, focused on nothing but beating the throw. Her foot hit the bag, and as soon as she stopped her forward momentum, she whirled around, looking for Carter to make that crucial safe-or-out call.

He made the call. But not at first base. The outfielder had thrown the ball home in an attempt to stop Principal Mullins from scoring.

Carter was wearing his sling, but the gesture he made with his one good arm was unmistakable, even to a baseball noob. As was the single word out of his mouth. *Safe.*

Principal Mullins had scored.

The game was over. Haven High had won.

Her colleagues were all whooping, dashing toward home plate to celebrate. Olive turned to jog toward them, saw Principal Mullins turning her way with a wide grin on his face, his hand extended for a high five. It was the sort of thing that Olive had been daydreaming about . . . well, for a few days.

She slapped her palm against her boss's, grinned as her coworkers patted her shoulder and helmet in excitement, but she didn't really see any of them. All of her attention was on one person. And his was on her.

Carter grinned. Olive grinned back. And giving in to the happiness bursting out of her, she acted before thinking, launching herself at Carter full force, wrapping her arms around his neck, her legs around his hips.

He laughed as he caught her and, even one-handed, easily supported her weight as he smiled up at her.

"Nice RBI, Dunn," he said.

"I know." Then she planted her palms on either side of his chiseled cheeks, and kissed Haven's very own golden boy, right on the mouth.

It was a spontaneous kiss, driven by instinct and pure glee. A playful kiss between friends.

Only, the second her lips touched his, something shifted, low in Olive's belly. And worse, deep in her heart. It was more than the hot pull of sexual awareness, though there was definitely that.

It was a whisper. A quiet voice uttering the simplest, and most powerful, of statements. *You belong here.*

Ignoring the voice and the heartache it promised, Olive let herself indulge in the kiss for only a moment before pulling back and forcing a bright grin.

But Carter didn't grin back, and the warmth in his eyes had nothing to do with friendship.

The arm around her tightened, and the fingers of his bad arm, sandwiched between them, found the fabric of her shirt, tugging her back toward him. The command in his gaze was unmistakable. *Again.*

Heart thumping in her chest, Olive's face started to lower to his.

And then she heard it. Instead of the jubilant celebrating, there were whispers. Real whispers this time, not just in her mind.

Olive turned her head, scanning the crowd to see what had happened.

Not *what*, she realized, as her stomach sank. *Who* had happened.

Felicity George was back, and Olive was unceremoniously dropped to her feet as Carter went to her.

The voice in her head had been only half-right. She very well may belong to Carter—but he most definitely did not belong to her.

Chapter Eighteen

"Felicity! Felicity, hold up," Carter yelled, a little exasperated as he jogged after the retreating brunette. "Would you *wait?*"

She did not wait, but Carter had the advantage. He was in tennis shoes, his ex in towering platform sandals. He caught up to her in the parking lot, and resigned, she turned around to face him. Carter drew up short, just before colliding into her.

He felt . . . stunned.

And a little numb.

Felicity looked the same as he remembered. *Exactly* the same. Same pink cheeks, wide eyes. Same slim shoulders, shy smile. Even her hairstyle was the same as in his memories, parted on the side and styled in loose waves down to the middle of her back.

The fact that she hadn't changed should have pleased him, but instead he felt strangely unsettled. People were supposed to change. Age. Evolve.

He knew he had.

"Hi, Carter." The voice, too, was the same. Soft, and just the slightest bit husky, as though she didn't use it often. And she hadn't, not around him. She'd always been fairly quiet. In that way, she was Olive's opposite.

Understatement. Felicity was Olive's opposite in every way.

Olive.

Thinking of her, Carter felt anything *but* numb. If Felicity had always made him feel content, Olive Dunn made him feel alive.

But now wasn't the time to think how Olive had felt in his arms just moments before, or the sweetness of her surprise kiss, or the way he wanted to repeat both experiences as soon as possible.

It would have to wait. Carter was long overdue for dealing with the woman in front of him. The one who'd brought him back to Haven in the first place, though the plan seemed silly now.

"Hi." He cleared his throat. "It's good to see you."

And it was. He couldn't deny that there was a sense of fondness as he looked at the woman who once had been a girl he'd loved. But that's all it was. Fondness.

She smiled and smoothed a nervous hand over the skirt of her strapless white dress, which was strangely formal for a hot summer Saturday at the high school softball field.

"How are you?" he asked when she said nothing.

"I'm fine. I'm great, actually. Recently divorced, which was a little brutal, but was the best thing for both of us."

He nodded awkwardly. "I'm glad things are good."

"And you?" she said, tilting her head. "You're dating Olive Dunn now?"

Olive.

Carter hesitated a second too long. "I gave her some pointers for the softball game."

Felicity's eyebrows lifted. "Looked like a bit more than softball pointers. She was all over you."

And I wanted to be all over her.

Carter felt a flicker of annoyance at Felicity's proprietary tone, and felt the urge to defend Olive, though God knew she was a woman who didn't need defending.

Before he could reply, Felicity let out a little laugh. "Oh my God, listen to me. I sound like a jealous girlfriend, over Olive, of all people. I lost the right to be possessive a long time ago. Didn't I?"

There was a slight searching note in her tone that told him the question wasn't as rhetorical as it should have been.

Yeah, you did.

He didn't say it, though. Carter had had plenty of experience in letting women down easy, but this wasn't just any woman—it was one he'd once pledged to *marry* if they were still single. He could only hope that she'd forgotten about it.

Her choice of an impractical white dress made him think that perhaps she hadn't.

"I hoped you'd be here. In town," she said in a soft, sweet voice as she held his gaze.

There was, again, a distinct hopeful note in her voice, and though Carter didn't want to hurt her, it was hard to feel much of anything around a grown-up Felicity who somehow seemed stuck in a time warp.

She gently reached out and touched her fingers to his sling. "I was sorry to hear about this. Did it hurt?"

A broken arm? Yeah.

Carter forced a smile. "Nothing a little ibuprofen couldn't take the edge off, and it's well on its way to healing. At least that's what I'm hoping the doctor will tell me on Monday morning when I go into the city for an appointment." It was a canned brush-off response. He didn't have even the slightest inclination to confide in Felicity the way he did Olive.

She frowned. "You're leaving? But I just got back."

And you haven't been the center of my universe in a long time, he thought uncharitably.

"It's been scheduled for a few weeks now," Carter said gently. "My bosses would be pissed if I cancel."

"Ah, well, I guess you're kind of important now," she said with a coy smile, her hand still on his arm. Felicity tilted her head toward the field. "Are you all finished up there? I'm not sure we'll have privacy for much longer once everyone starts going to their cars. I was thinking we could grab a drink or a coffee or something . . . catch up?"

"I'd love to," Carter said. "But I'd planned to drive down to the city tonight."

He'd been planning no such thing. But he needed room to think. To figure out why, after weeks of waiting for this moment, he couldn't stop thinking about Olive's lips against his. And what he wanted to do about that.

"Oh." Her hand dropped. "Okay. Can you drive? You know, with your arm?"

"I'll manage. There's no law against people with one arm behind the wheel. Rain check on that coffee?" he said with a smile to soften the blow of rejection.

She smiled back. "That sounds great. We have . . . *things* to talk about."

And there it was. If there had been any doubt that Felicity remembered their pact, that it was the reason she was back, it disappeared when she held his gaze for a meaningfully long moment.

"Yeah. We do," he said, reaching out and giving her hand a friendly squeeze. "It was good to see you again, Felicity."

Her eyes flickered with disappointment as he dropped her hand immediately and she undoubtedly heard the generic friendliness of his tone.

It wasn't a lie. He was glad that he'd seen her. But not for the reasons he'd expected.

Carter made it to his truck before he gave in to the urge to scan the slowly growing crowd for Olive.

He didn't see her. Told himself he was glad. And *that* was the lie.

Olive said a distracted thank-you to whoever refilled her glass from one of the many beer pitchers being passed around as she checked her phone for the hundredth time.

Another text from Kelly. One from her cousin, Sarah, who'd been at the game. One from her aunt, asking whether her phone prompting her to upgrade software was a "hack."

Nothing from Carter.

The Haven High staff, and what felt like half the team, had headed to Abby's Sports Bar after the game, and though the mood was decidedly jubilant, Olive hadn't been able to muster more than fake laughs and smiles.

Someone dropped into the seat beside her. "Do you want to talk about it?"

Olive took a sip of her beer and gave Kelly Blakely a look out of the corner of her eye. "What do *you* think?"

Her friend smiled, though her gaze was concerned. "I think I saw you kiss Carter Ramsey, and then he ran after his ex-girlfriend."

"It was technically a kiss, in that my mouth touched his mouth, but it wasn't *that* kind of kiss."

Lies. Lies. Lies.

Kelly looked at her skeptically.

"We're just friends," Olive said, the sentence sounding . . . wrong. They were friends, but after that kiss, there was nothing *just* about it, at least on her end.

"Friends who've been spending a lot of time together. I know Mark and I've been in the city the past couple weeks, but since we've been back, everyone I've talked to has said you and Carter are inseparable."

"He's helping me with the reunion."

"And teaching you to play softball?"

"We're just helping each other out."

Kelly helped herself to the stack of pint glasses in the middle of the table, as well as one of the pitchers of beer. "You do remember who you're talking to, right?"

"My very annoying, very nosy friend?"

"Your very *caring* friend, who's invested in your happiness. And, if I may be so bold, knows a hell of a lot more about what's going on between you and Carter than you do."

"How do you even remotely figure that?"

Kelly smiled. "You do remember how Mark and I got together, right?"

"Of course. It's Haven's most epic love story."

Kelly and Mark had been best friends forever, and Kelly had been just about the only person who didn't know he was in love with her. It had taken a psychic, a parade of her ex-boyfriends, and a little Christmas magic to get Kelly to see what was right in front of her.

Though if Carter and Felicity made good on their marriage pact and lived happily ever after, Kelly and Mark would have to make room for a tie as the town's most legendary fairy tale.

"Exactly my point," Kelly said. "Mark and I are a love story that started out as 'just friends,' so I know a little something about the line you're trying to feed me right now."

"Carter and I aren't you and Mark," Olive protested. "For starters, we barely knew each other in high school. We're friends now, sure, but we've really only known each other for a couple weeks. We're just neighbors. We help each other out—"

"You *kiss*," Kelly interjected.

"It wasn't like a *Twilight* kiss, more like a playful smack."

"Liv, if your bar for epic kisses is a teen movie about vampires, we really need to find you a man."

I think I've found one.

The thought was ridiculous. She didn't want Carter Ramsey. Or rather she did, but in a fleeting, impractical kind of way. There was no room for a pro-athlete, magazine-cover pretty boy in her life. They lived in two different universes, and their paths were crossing for only the briefest period of time, and only because he was back in town for Felicity.

She picked up her phone again. No new messages.

"They're not together," Kelly said gently. "Felicity and Carter."

Olive spun her head around to look at her friend. "How do you know?"

"Mark and I saw Carter drive away. Alone."

The relief that flooded through her was so intense she didn't know what to do with it. With a groan, Olive stacked her palms on the table and leaned over until her forehead rested on the backs of her hands.

"Oh, honey," Kelly said quietly, stroking Olive's ponytail. "You really like him."

"Maybe," Olive said, her voice muffled. "I don't know."

"I think you do."

Olive lifted her head. "No. I don't. I've never really done this before. My relationships, even the long-term ones, have been super blah. I've never felt that *thing*."

"And you feel it for Carter?" Kelly asked, keeping her voice low.

"I don't know," Olive said honestly. "It's nothing . . . It's not at all what I thought it would feel like."

"How so?" Kelly sipped her beer.

"Shouldn't it feel . . . *nice* when you think about the other person?" Olive asked.

"What's it feel like?"

"Sort of like a roller coaster," Olive said. "The kind where you feel like you're going to puke, but then for some stupid reason, you still want to do it all over again. And I don't even like roller coasters."

"You don't?" Kelly looked surprised. "For some reason I definitely see you as a roller-coaster person."

Olive shook her head. "No control. Now if I got to *drive* the roller coaster . . ."

Kelly looked like she wanted to say something, but instead pressed her lips together and took another sip of beer. "How does Carter feel about you?"

"Well, I think the fact that he literally dropped me *in the dirt* to chase after Felicity pretty much says it all."

"Hmm." Kelly tapped her nails on the table. "So, I hate to play the *as someone who's been married for four years* card, but as someone who's been married for four years, one thing I've learned is that you definitely can't predict what men are thinking. The only way to get inside their head is to sit them down and pry it out of them."

"Ah, but see," Olive said lightly. "What if I don't really want to know what's going on in Carter's head?"

What if I don't like what I find?

"But—"

"New plan," Olive interrupted, picking up her glass and clinking it to Kelly's. "We forget all about him. Or at the very least, remember that in just a couple weeks, he'll be gone. And I won't see him for another ten years, by which time, he'll be thrice divorced, his model ex-wives having taken all of his money. He'll be in denial that he's gained weight, so his jeans will be too small, and he'll forever be hiking them up to try and cover the beer belly that's spilling over. It'll be like his thing—his tic. Oh, and his hair will have begun to thin in a very strange pattern, and he'll wear it in a weird, creepy ponytail."

Kelly wrinkled her nose skeptically. "I kind of don't think—"

"Shh, shh, shh," Olive said, putting a finger over her friend's mouth. "We're all allowed our fantasies, and that is mine. Now. Let's have another beer, eat some nachos, and not think about Carter Ramsey for the rest of the night."

And Olive succeeded, by sheer force of will. Sort of. She definitely didn't check the door every five minutes to see if he'd come to join in the victory party. She *definitely* didn't check her phone for a message that never came.

And when the Haven High volleyball coach and self-appointed designated driver dropped Olive off at home a couple of hours later, she didn't care that Carter's truck wasn't in his driveway.

She definitely didn't wonder where he was. Or who he was with.

She definitely didn't stay up all night wondering.

Chapter Nineteen

The doctor's prognosis had been shit. Not completely unexpected, but still shit.

And though it had been almost three weeks since he'd last been home, and he'd have thought that's where he'd want to go to wallow in the news . . .

Nope.

The penthouse he'd lived in for the better part of five years didn't *feel* like home. It didn't matter that he'd slept in the place after every home game for nearly half a decade, or that all of his stuff was here, or that the doormen greeted him by name. It was familiar, yes, but the familiarity provided no comfort, no relief in returning to one's place of residence after a long trip.

Worst of all, the swanky apartment did nothing to clear his head and had done nothing to the pensive restlessness he'd felt ever since the softball game on Saturday.

Carter told himself he just needed time to readjust to life in the city, to remember that *this* was his life. An enormous big screen, a state-of-the-art home gym, a brilliant, vibrant city where he could have anything he wanted delivered in a matter of minutes.

He didn't want any of that. He wanted his dumpy, impersonal rental home, the warmth of Cedar & Salt or his mother's kitchen. He wanted the stupid red truck he'd become rather attached to. He wanted the noisy high school biology teacher he'd become *very* attached to.

Not forever, he knew that. He and Olive didn't just live in different cities; they lived in different *worlds*. When he got off the Injured List and returned to his old routine, he didn't know how he'd even be able to see her, much less be with her.

But just because they couldn't have forever didn't mean they couldn't have right now. Right? Carter had no idea. But he knew someone who gave some pretty good advice and was only a short drive away.

Following his doctor's appointment, Mike dropped Carter off at his apartment, and instead of pulling out the key fob to let him in his front door, he pulled a different key out of his pocket.

Ten minutes later, he was in his red truck, on his way back to Haven.

The two-hour drive gave him a chance to make a phone call he was dreading, but also eager to get over with. Using Jody's Bluetooth (he'd somehow found himself following Billy's and Olive's lead in calling the car by her given name), he called his agent to deliver the news, followed by another, even more difficult, conversation with the team manager and a couple of his closest teammates.

Nobody was happy. Nobody was particularly surprised, either. He was nearly twenty-nine, not twenty-three. When it came to injuries, that made a difference.

Luckily, most of the morning-commute traffic had dissipated by the time Carter was on the road, and he made it back to the Hudson Valley in record time. Carter pulled into his parents' driveway and prayed his mom would be home.

His parents, like Olive, rarely locked their front door, but not wanting to startle his mother if she was home, he knocked. She opened the door moments later, blinking only once in surprise, and then, with a mother's intuition that everything was not okay, ushered him inside and gave him a long, warm hug that was exactly what he needed.

"Come," she said, speaking for the first time, already heading into the kitchen. "I'm making you your favorite lunch."

"Which is?" he asked, not realizing he *had* a favorite lunch.

"Grilled cheese and tomato soup," she said, opening the fridge. She pointed a commanding finger at the kitchen table. "Sit."

He smiled as he obeyed. He hadn't had grilled cheese and tomato soup in years, but he'd loved it as a kid. And if he was ever in need of a sodium-heavy, carb-and-fat-focused comfort meal, it was now.

"Cheddar or swiss?" she asked, her head buried in the fridge.

"You choose."

"Both," she said, straightening with grilled-cheese supplies in hand. "When someone looks like you look, two cheeses is always the answer."

"How do I look?" he asked, pretty sure he didn't want to know.

"Like you didn't sleep at all. I *told* you renting a house was risky. You never know what kind of mattress they purchase, the linens aren't your own . . ."

"Actually, I slept at my place last night."

She turned around in surprise, two bread slices in hand. "You've already been to the city and back? It's barely noon!"

"I headed down Saturday night. Had an early doctor's appointment this morning."

"The doctor?" Her gaze dropped to his sling. "Oh. *Oh.*"

"Yeah."

She set the bread on the cutting board and came to sit at the table beside him. "Was it not good news?"

"No. It wasn't."

"Oh, Carter." His mom's face crumpled. "It's not healing like they thought?"

"It's healing fine. The X-ray showed all good things," he said, running his hand through his hair. "In fact, they said the cast'll come off next week."

His mom gave a reassuring smile. "That's good. Right?"

Carter exhaled. "They scheduled surgery."

"But if the X-ray was good—"

"My shoulder's busted, Mom. It was even before the fall, we just didn't know until this." He lifted his cast.

"And this shoulder injury. It's serious?"

"Yeah. Well, not debilitating. For anyone else, it wouldn't be that big a deal. Surgery. Let it heal. Go back to normal life."

"But it's not that way for you?"

Carter stared blindly at the cheerful yellow flowers in the center of the table. "Depends. Sometimes it heals on its own, and you've got a decent chance of returning to normal play. Sometimes it requires surgery, and you've got a less-than-decent chance of returning to normal play. I fall in the latter category."

He dragged his hand over his face. "I don't want to just *play*. I want to be as good as I was."

That's who Carter Ramsey is. The best. *Without that label . . .*

"Who's to say you won't be?" Tracy said with a mother's optimistic confidence that her son could do *anything*. "It may take time, but you've always been the hardest-working person I know."

"Well, that's another part of the problem," he said, forcing a smile. "Time wasn't exactly on my side even before the accident."

"What do you mean? You're only in your twenties!"

"I turn twenty-nine next month," he reminded her needlessly, since moms tended to know that sort of detail. "It's not ancient by MLB standards, but I'm no longer one of the young guys, either. Even with nonstop therapy in the off-season, I won't be able to start next season, at least not in the majors. By the time I return—*if* I return—I'll be thirty."

"Thirty is the new twenty," she said, patting his good arm.

"Not in pro sports."

Her smile dimmed. "Oh, Carter. How long have you known about this shoulder thing?"

"A while."

"Why didn't you say anything to anyone?"

I did.

Carter thought of Olive—the one person he *had* told—then pushed the thought aside. One problem at a time.

"I guess I've been trying to sort out how I feel about it."

"And? How do you feel?"

He blew out a breath. "Conflicted. I hate the thought of not getting that World Series ring before my career's up. And yet . . ."

For the first time in my life, I think I can catch a glimpse of life after baseball.

Trouble was, the vision flitted away before he could get a really good look at what he was doing, where he was. Who he was with.

Not that it was an easy concept to reconcile. He loved baseball more than just about anything.

But every ballplayer has their prime. Some peak early. Some are average. A rare few are late bloomers in their thirties. Carter was highly aware that he was in the "peaked early" category. Not that he resented his stint as Rookie of the Year and American League MVP, or all of his other accolades. But in his gut, he knew that thirtysomething Carter Ramsey would be very different from twentysomething Carter Ramsey on the field.

"I guess I'm still sorting it out," he told his mom.

She nodded, seeming to sense he wasn't quite ready to talk about it. "All right. How about a subject change?" she said brightly.

He groaned, already guessing what she wanted to change the subject to.

"Sooooo, Felicity's back," she said in a chipper tone.

He'd guessed correctly. "Yeah. I saw her."

"Oh, I know. What I don't know—what nobody knows—is why Felicity saw you kissing Olive Dunn."

The vividness of the memory—the sheer sweetness of the moment—washed over him and pushed back against the doom and gloom of his impending surgery. Still he kept his face carefully neutral and merely smiled at his mother.

"Are you and Olive . . ." His mom lifted her eyebrows.

"We're friends."

"I see. And you and Felicity?" his mom asked, returning to the stove to resume making the grilled cheese.

"We're former high school sweethearts with fond memories, and that's all we'll ever be," he said, finally voicing aloud what he'd known for a while now.

"Does she know that?"

"We still need to talk. I don't know that it'll be an easy conversation, but I think Felicity will agree." He hoped.

"Well, I'm glad to hear it, but Felicity's not the *she* I was referring to," his mother said without turning around.

Olive.

No, Olive didn't know what Felicity was to him.

She would. But there was something he needed to do first.

Chapter Twenty

Tuesday, August 25

"I could have sworn Carter's supposed to be helping you with this nonsense," Caitlyn said, scowling down at the sheet of name tags in her lap, then rubbing at the Sharpie ink on the side of her hand.

"Your brother and I are taking some time apart right now," Olive said casually from her chair next to Caitlyn's bed, as she wrote Belinda Harmon's name on a blank tag.

"Huh," Caitlyn said. "Does he know that?"

"Does who know what?" Olive asked, blowing on the ink. She was already regretting recruiting Caitlyn to help her instead of Kelly. She'd thought the activity would distract the increasingly testy Caitlyn from her bed rest boredom, but being around Carter's twin made Olive think about Carter more than she wanted to.

Caitlyn also had *really* crappy handwriting.

"Does Carter know you're taking some time apart?" Caitlyn pressed, not even pretending to help with the name tags anymore.

"Well, he should. I've done a bang-up job of avoiding him, including keeping all the blinds closed in my house."

"Very mature approach, I like it. But *what* is going on with you two?" Caitlyn asked.

"You heard about the kiss?" Olive asked, somewhat rhetorically. "And Felicity?"

"From just about everyone I know, yeah. Apparently it was *hot*. And then immediately awkward when Felicity showed up."

"It wasn't like we Frenched," Olive grumbled. "The kiss lasted two seconds."

"Frenched?" Caitlyn said with a laugh. "How old are you? And sure, sure, it was quick and playful. And, *oh yeah*, your legs were wrapped around his waist, and his hands were on your butt."

Olive made an irritated noise. "You weren't even there!"

"Come on. You know the nature of this town more than anyone. I had no fewer than twenty people describe the kiss in *very* intriguing detail to poor *bed rested, miss all the good stuff* me. Which may have actually been a blessing, seeing as it's my brother we're talking about. But still, if you're actively avoiding him, it must mean things are . . . complicated?"

Caitlyn's voice softened slightly, and Olive knew that though she was fiercely loyal to her brother, she was also her friend and would listen, if she needed to talk.

Olive wished she *could* talk it out. She just wasn't entirely sure what to say.

"*Complicated* about sums it up," Olive said, forcing a smile.

Caitlyn sighed and set her palm on her stomach, rubbing absently for several seconds before speaking again. "Olive, I feel like I need to apologize."

"It better not be for the bed rest thing again."

"No, not that. But I shouldn't have pushed you and Carter together for the reunion thing. It didn't really occur to me that it would end up this way."

Olive couldn't help it. She flinched at the reminder that nobody, not even one of her closest friends, could imagine a world where Carter *might* be into someone like her.

Not that he was into her. But still, the way he'd looked at her on the field . . .

Just heat of the moment. A heat he probably assuaged later with Felicity.

"It was really nothing," Olive said, feeling like a broken record as she started writing on another name tag. "I've had blinks last longer than that kiss."

"It's not just that," Caitlyn said, plucking at the comforter in agitation. "Carter wouldn't even be in town if it weren't for me dangling Felicity's divorce and return to Haven in front of him."

This time Olive caught the flinch in time, but *damn*, Caitlyn was delivering a lot of unintentional jabs here. Olive didn't want to be reminded that she and Carter were an unlikely pairing. Or that he and Felicity were a very likely pairing.

"It worked, didn't it?" Olive said, placing the cap back on the marker with more force than necessary. "He's here. And now she's here. Everybody wins."

"You don't," Caitlyn said softly.

Olive was already shaking her head. "I'm exactly the same as I've ever been. Perfectly happy with my choices in life. I have my dream career, I'm living in the town I grew up in, which I love. I have amazing friends, I own my own house, I know how to change my own tire and grill my own steaks, and none of that changes just because your brother decided to kill time with me as his source of amusement until his lady love arrived."

Caitlyn rubbed her stomach again as she studied Olive. "That was a lot of information."

Olive shrugged. She'd meant every word. She *was* happy. She *had* been happy before Carter strolled into town. And she would be happy again after he left. So what if in the in-between time she was feeling a little . . . confused.

"What if I were to tell you that I don't think Felicity is right for him?" Caitlyn said.

"I'd tell you that it's none of my business. And that maybe you should have thought that through before using her to get him to come back to Haven," Olive couldn't resist adding.

"I know," Caitlyn said glumly. "I just missed him. A couple of days at Christmas and box seats to his games a couple times a year isn't the same as when he lived down the hall and I could go to him for everything."

Olive's hand paused in the process of writing out another name tag. Caitlyn's words hit a raw spot, because Olive had learned exactly what it was like to have Carter within shouting distance. And the past couple of days, she'd also learned the pain that came with having that taken away.

It was a pain she should get used to, since after the reunion, he'd be gone for good.

"You should tell Carter that," Olive said, finishing the last sheet of name tags and beginning to gather their supplies. "Let him know you miss him and want to see him more often. And next time, leave his ex out of it."

"Aha!" Caitlyn's eyes lit up. "Did you hear your tone just then? *Snippy*. You *do* hate that she's here."

"Not that she's here," Olive said, choosing her words carefully. *It's the reason that she's here.*

As far as Olive knew, Carter still hadn't mentioned to his family about his and Felicity's stupid ten-year marriage pact. She didn't actually think they could be so stupid as to assume they'd still be compatible enough for marriage simply because they'd had some sweet puppy love in their teens.

But then, what did she know about relationships, or love, for that matter? Maybe it really was like the movies, and some people were simply meant to be. Maybe they could lock eyes after years apart and immediately resurrect their soul mate status. Wasn't that how it worked in *The Notebook*?

Come to think of it, she never had liked that movie as much as everybody else. Sofia had made her watch it, then had been scandalized when Olive hadn't cried: *"If that movie doesn't make you cry, nothing will."* Olive had shrugged—she simply wasn't wired that way.

Saying goodbye to Caitlyn, Olive loaded the name tag supplies into her car and then decided to leave Bingo at Caitlyn and AJ's and walk to the next item on her to-do list to get some fresh air.

She was halfway down Franklin Street, nearly to the florist, when she passed by SherryLee's coffee shop. There, sitting at the table by the window, in plain view for everyone to see, were Carter and Felicity.

Holding hands.

Olive reversed course before either could see her and managed to make it back to her car before she proved Sofia wrong.

Olive could cry after all.

◆　◆　◆

Carter was grinning as he jogged up the steps to Olive's house, bottle of Zinfandel in hand. He also had picked up a pan of what his mother had assured him was the best lasagna in town—other than her own—but he'd left it in his refrigerator to be retrieved later, on account of the whole one-arm thing.

Even with the annoyance of still being hampered by his injury, even with the surgery on the calendar and the iffy prognosis that came with it, Carter felt the lightest he had in weeks as he reached for Olive's doorknob to open it without knocking, as had become second nature over the past couple of weeks.

Carter's smile faded slightly when he found it locked.

Impatient to see her, he tucked the wine bottle under his slinged arm and knocked. There was no answer, so he gave it a second before knocking again. Bingo was in the driveway, so he knew she was home.

"Hey, Olive," he called when, after another knock, she still didn't respond. He rattled the doorknob.

"Take the hint, dude!"

Carter started in surprise when he heard her voice, sounding as though it was directly on the other side of the door. Carter felt an unexpected flicker of hurt at the realization that she'd become the one person he could never wait to see, the one person he'd *never* close his door to. And that the feeling was apparently not mutual.

"What's wrong?" he asked softly, already wanting to fix it.

"Nothing. Go away."

He frowned. The Olive he knew was not the type to hide when something was bothering her. And definitely not the type to lie.

"What happened to 'this is Haven, we don't lock doors'?" he said, twisting the door handle again, futilely.

"That was before there were unwanted men on this block."

Again, the flash of hurt, though at least now he had confirmation that he was at the crux of what was pissing her off. And, if he was really honest with himself, it was deserved. He had been avoiding her since the softball game, needing to sort things out, first in his own head, then with his mother, then, perhaps most crucially, with Felicity.

"Look, Olive," he tried. "I know that things were weird after the game."

"Oh, you mean when you dropped me in the dirt, and then chased after your ex?"

Carter flinched, then rested his forehead against her front door, frustrated. "It wasn't what you think—"

The door yanked open, and he nearly fell forward, but her palm found the center of his chest, not in a gentle-caress kind of way, but in a firm, back-the-hell-up kind of way.

"Really?" she said. "Which part wasn't what I thought? That I kissed you, and you promptly dropped me to go after the woman you pledged to marry if you were both single? Or that you disappeared completely after that?"

Carter understood her anger—he regretted it. But he also felt a little surge of elation at the fact that she cared.

Still glaring at him, her eyes dropped to the wine still tucked beneath his arm. She reached out and tugged it, tucking it under her own arm. "Thank you. Bye."

Carter laughed in disbelief. "Seriously? Can't we just—"

"What did you think, Carter?" she interrupted. "That Felicity would come back into town, you guys would pick up where you left off, and you and I would pick up where we left off? It's different now. I'm happy for you two, but I don't have any interest in being the third wheel to your love story."

"You're getting it wrong," Carter said, frustrated.

She sighed wearily and leaned against the doorway. "How so?"

He swallowed. He had no idea what he wanted to say. It's not as though he and Olive were going to ride off into the sunset. He'd be gone in a couple of weeks, and she'd be right here, same as she'd always been. She had no interest in being a pro baseball player's girlfriend, and he didn't know how to be a high school teacher's boyfriend.

He didn't even want that.

Did he?

"Yeah, okay then. Good talk," she said dismissively, starting to close the door again.

He reached out and slammed the door open, and just started talking. "I'm sorry I left you after the game. I wasn't expecting her. It was a knee-jerk reaction, but—"

"It's *fine*, Carter," Olive said, the resignation in her voice making him panic.

But it wasn't fine. For the first time since she'd opened the door, he looked at her—really looked at her—and saw what he'd missed before. The slight red around her eyes and nose.

Olive Dunn had been crying.

Over him?

The selfish, possessive part of him wanted it to be so. The friend in him ached at the thought.

He reached out to touch her cheek, but she jerked back, slapping his hand at the same time. Carter nearly smiled, but her next words erased the urge.

"I saw you," she said quietly. "This afternoon, the two of you at SherryLee's. Holding hands."

His stomach dropped, because he knew exactly how that must have looked. "It wasn't what you think," he said quickly.

"I don't really care. I wish you guys all sorts of cute babies."

She started to close the door again, and this time he blocked it with his body. "I'm not having babies with Felicity. I'm not doing anything with Felicity. I'm here, Olive," Carter said a little desperately. "Standing on *your* front doorstep."

Olive rested her cheek on the side of the door. "I do still want to be your friend, Carter. I just need a day."

Friend. Carter realized in that moment one didn't explain things to an irate Olive Dunn. They showed her.

Acting on instinct and weeks' worth of building attraction, Carter stepped toward her, closing the distance between them.

He took his time lowering his head, letting his lips move over hers with enough gentleness not to scare her away, but enough urgency to let her know that friendship didn't have a damn thing to do with his reason for being here at this moment.

She didn't kiss him back, but neither did she move away. She stood perfectly still, as though thinking through the pros and cons of his nearness, and had he not been so turned on, he might have smiled because it was exactly the way he'd expect a biology teacher with Olive's brain to do things.

Carter lifted his head, but didn't step back. He wanted her. But the next move had to be Olive's.

He held his breath as he rested his cheek against hers, hoping he hadn't destroyed everything they'd built by kissing her. But he also knew if he and Olive didn't confront the heat between them, he'd regret it long after he left Haven.

Still, she didn't move, and just as Carter's heart began to sink in realization that she didn't feel the same way—that he'd imagined the pull between them—Olive lifted her hands to his face and set her lips against his.

Chapter Twenty-One

Tuesday, August 25

Olive had never really understood the concept of losing oneself in lust. She'd seen it in movies. She'd read about it in books. She'd heard Kelly describe it in far more detail than she'd ever really wanted to hear about her friends.

And though she understood that sort of primal reaction on an academic level—they were all animals, after all—she'd never experienced it.

She'd never even *hoped* to experience it, having decided after a string of meh sexual encounters that perhaps she wasn't wired that way. Or perhaps, more likely, she simply didn't inspire that reaction in men.

In kissing Carter, Olive realized her error. It wasn't that she wasn't built that way, or that men didn't feel that way. It was just that she hadn't been with the right man. *This* man.

For a long, gratifying moment, Carter simply let her kiss him—he let her discover and enjoy him, her palms becoming accustomed to the hard planes of his face, her fingers learning the texture of his hair, her mouth discovering that he tasted like mint and man.

But then she bit his bottom lip, and his control snapped. He stepped all the way into her foyer, kicked her front door shut, and a second later had Olive pinned against that same door, his hand braced next to her head as he tilted his head and crushed his mouth to hers in a kiss that left her breathless.

Olive's hands slid to his waist, fingers greedily pulling at his shirt, needing him closer. Carter groaned, the hand he'd braced on her door sliding down to cup her face, tilting her head back, his tongue plunging deep.

The last man she'd kissed had been about her height, but Carter had a few inches on her, and years of turning his body into a high-performance machine had made him wonderfully broad and hard. For the first time in her life, Olive understood what it meant to feel fully woman. Understood that it wasn't about strength and weakness, or big and small, but simply male to female. Want to want.

Olive bit his lip again, and he rewarded her with another aroused groan, followed almost immediately by a sound of irritated pain.

"What's wrong?" she asked when he pulled back, breathing hard as he frowned down at her.

"I've hated this fucking sling from the very beginning, but never as much as at this moment," he said, his lone good hand sliding from her face, over her shoulder, and down to her waist, his gaze raking over her body as though it were killing him to have only one hand to explore her with.

Some little devil nudged Olive on, and instead of sympathizing, she tortured him further, easing him back slightly so that her hands could grip the hem of her tank top. Holding his gaze, she tugged the shirt upward, up and over her head, tossing it aside and standing before him in only a black bra.

Carter's breath whooshed out as he looked down at her, and Olive felt a rush of feminine power. She may not be experienced at this, but she knew when a man wanted her, and even if it weren't for the bulge at the front of his jeans, the heat of Carter Ramsey's gaze told her that he wanted to be here.

Wanted her.

"God, Olive," he murmured, lifting his hand and brushing the backs of his fingers over the swells of her breasts.

This time it was her breath that left her on a gust, and he gave her a knowing look before slipping his fingers beneath the fabric, almost but not quite grazing her nipple. Her back arched of its own accord, wanting more, and he gave her a wicked smile, continuing his teasing strokes.

"I hate you," she managed as his lips found her throat.

"I know." His fingers slipped lower, brushing against her nipple, and he smiled against her neck when she cried out.

Over and over, his fingers played with her, his movements hampered by the tight fabric, until he'd finally had enough and removed his hand, sliding it to her back. She frowned in protest at the loss of his hand on her breast, and was just about to join his complaining about his splint when her bra slipped free, his adept fingers having managed the clasp one-handed.

She freed herself as Carter's mouth moved from her neck down to her collarbone, his teeth nipping just hard enough to thrill before he bent down farther, his mouth hovering above the tip of her breast for a torturous heartbeat, before his tongue licked over her in a teasing flick.

Olive let out a desperate cry as she arched into him. His lips closed over her nipple, warm and wet as he stroked her with his tongue in a hot swirling motion that made her see stars. His hand played with her other breast, and then he returned to the first, back and forth, until she could barely remember her own name.

Carter's hand slid to the waistband of her shorts, and then he scowled up at her. "Of all the days you don't wear your gym shorts."

"What?" she asked, wits still scattered.

"Well," he said, knees unbending as he straightened and pressed a kiss to her mouth, "if it weren't for this damn button and zipper, my hand could be down your shorts right now, where I'm guessing my fingers would find you wet." His palm slid down, cupping her, and she gasped.

Her eyes closed, her head pressing back against the door, she was trying to clear her mind and get control of the situation, but it was so hard when he was stroking her through the shorts, the air cool on her breasts, still wet from his mouth.

"Help me out with this damn button, and it'll be worth your while," he said with a smile against her cheek as his free hand tugged impatiently at her jean shorts.

Control was overrated.

Taking a deep breath, she lifted her eyes to his and did as he asked, her fingers fumbling only a little as she undid the button, the sound of the zipper rasp almost electric.

His fingers found her blue boy short–cut underwear. It didn't even pretend to match her bra, but he didn't seem to care. Not when he traced his fingers over the front of the fabric, and not when he moved his hand up slightly, then back down, under the fabric . . .

They both moaned when his fingers found her wet and ready for him.

"I knew it," Carter said huskily, his fingers sliding over her, exploring at first, then more deliberately, stroking her clit in torturous circles before moving down to push a finger inside her.

Olive's fingers dug into his shoulders as she fought against the climax, not wanting the moment to end even as she needed release.

He slid another finger into her, pushing her ever closer to the edge, and somehow she found the willpower to grip his wrist. "Wait."

He stilled immediately. "You want me to stop?"

"Not even close," she said gently, easing him away from her slightly as her fingers dropped to his shoulder. "Now, let's see if this damn sling is as easy to get off as it was to get on."

It was, soon going the way of her bra on her floor. His shirt was harder, having to go up and over his head without jarring his shoulder or cast, but the struggle was worth it.

She'd already seen Carter shirtless that day in the bathroom when she'd helped him with the sling, but having him shirtless and hers to touch was heaven.

Her fingers boldly explored the hard planes of his chest, the defined grooves of his abs, the broad, firm expanse of his back, her short nails dragging down slightly on either side of his spine as he let her investigate every inch of his exposed skin.

She wanted more.

His lips caressed her ear as his hand stroked the curve of her waist. "If I could, I'd carry you to the bed, but given the circumstances . . ."

"Maybe some other time," she said with a smile, even as a little part of her heart acknowledged that there was unlikely to be another time. Or at least very many.

She led him upstairs, though it took five times longer than it should have because they kept stopping to make out like a couple of horny teenagers.

Finally inside her bedroom, Olive went to her toes to press her mouth against his, moving her fingers down to the fly of his jeans, flicking the button open. He exhaled against her mouth as her palm slid into his open fly, rubbing the straining bulge beneath his boxers.

Carter kicked off his shoes, and together, they wrangled his jeans down and off until she was staring at Carter Ramsey wearing nothing but green boxers and a cast.

"Real people don't look like this," she muttered, her hands on his waist as she looked him up and down.

"Trust me. I'm as real as it gets," he said, wrapping his casted arm gently around her waist. His other hand brushed her hair from her face, the gesture almost tender as he pulled her against him for a searing, possessive kiss that made her feel achingly wanted.

Achingly his.

He pulled back, breathing hard, looking down at her bare breasts, his hand sliding down her stomach, hooking a finger into her underwear before his gaze came up again. "Tell me you have a condom."

"Ah." Her mind went blank. "Maybe?" Her heart sank, as she mentally went through the contents of her nightstand. Once upon a time, for a flash-in-the-pan boyfriend, she'd probably had a box, but she was pretty sure it was long gone.

"Hold on," he said, stepping back. "Hold the fuck on."

He bent, rummaging in his jeans for his wallet, his fingers gratifyingly shaky as he opened it, riffling through the contents.

He pulled out a foil packet with a grin.

She laughed at his boyishly triumphant expression. "What is this, high school?"

"God, I hope not," he muttered. "I was an idiot in high school. Missed out on all the good girls."

His playful words touched a part of her heart so deeply, she thought she might crack.

"Off," he said, pointing at the underwear she was still wearing.

"Off," she echoed, pointing at the boxers he was still wearing.

With two hands, she was faster, and reached out to help hurry him along until finally they were both naked and he was nudging her back on the bed, his body lowering to cover hers.

"Is this okay?" she asked, with a wary glance at the cast propped up along the side of her face.

"*Okay* doesn't even begin to cover it," he said, tearing open the condom with his teeth and maneuvering it on one-handed with ease. His knee nudged her legs apart as he settled all the way over her, his eyes searching her face, looking slightly stunned. "Your body fits mine so perfectly."

And then he proved exactly how perfectly they fit, sliding inside her.

Olive wanted to watch his face, wanted to commit the moment to memory, but then he began to move, and her eyes closed in need, her legs wrapping around his waist, as he murmured words she couldn't make out over the roaring in her own ears.

This was why people made such a big deal about sex, she realized, as reality seemed to get a little further away from her with each stroke, with each brush of his hand, his lips . . .

This was why people made such a big deal about lo—

Carter took her over the ledge before the thought could take hold, capturing her cries with his mouth.

Her body still clenching around his, Carter plunged his hand into her hair, fingers tangling into the strands as he thrust firmly into her one last time, his body bucking as he groaned into her neck.

Finally, their bodies relaxed, slowly, together, as he lowered atop her, his weight warm and welcome.

She kissed his injured shoulder, smiling at the slightly salty taste of him.

Carter made a muffled noise against her neck, something that might have been *I'll move in a minute.*

But she was in no hurry. She wrapped her arms around Carter Ramsey and would hold on as long as she had him.

Which wouldn't be long at all.

Her smile faded as reality settled through the rose-colored orgasmic fog.

Chapter Twenty-Two

Carter sat at his kitchen table, beer in hand, feet propped on the chair next to him, as he flicked down the papers he was holding so he could see Olive over the top.

"Be honest," he said, taking a sip of the beer. "Did you seduce me the other day so I'd help you mark these RSVPs?"

She looked at him over the top of the RSVP card she'd just pulled out of an envelope and gave him a smug smile.

"At least you fed me," he said with a fake sigh, eyeing the box of pizza. He contemplated another piece and decided against it. He had very specific plans for the rest of his evening with Olive, and they'd be better served without an extra helping of bread, sausage grease, and mozzarella.

First, though, they had to go through the stack of reunion RSVP cards that had been mailed to Olive's house.

"Remind me again, what year is it?" Carter said. "Don't they do this stuff electronically these days?"

"You can blame your sister for that," Olive said. "She insisted that sending out old-fashioned paper invitations was classier."

"And yet, Caitlyn's not here," Carter grumbled.

"Do you really want her to be?" Olive said slyly. "I'd have to put on pants."

"Excellent point," he said, reaching under the table to find her bare knee.

"Ah ah." She swatted his hand. "We have to finish these first. Ugh, we should have gone with the ones without glitter." She wiped her fingers futilely on one of the discarded envelopes.

The mention of glitter reminded him of their first meeting—well, their first meeting this decade—and he smiled at the memory. Who would have thought that he and the green-glitter woman next door would end up here, postcoitus, and headed toward round three for the day if Carter had his way?

"Do you still have that green glitter?" he asked.

Her eyes narrowed. "Why?"

"No reason." The thought of a naked Olive covered in glitter was strangely arousing. For that matter, the thought of Olive naked in any capacity was arousing.

Carter shifted uncomfortably in his chair. There was sex, and then there was whatever she'd been doing to him—with him—the past couple of days.

He didn't think it had a name, but the closest he could come up with was *heaven*.

"Do I even want to know what you're thinking right now?" she asked with a knowing smile.

"Let's just say you need to start reading those names faster," he said, reluctantly turning his attention back to checking names off the list.

It took them about a half hour to finish the rest of the cards, and after the final envelope was in the box, Olive tossed the last RSVP on the table. "Done. And we have a lot more people coming than I expected. Nearly the entire class. Your sister was right about your presence being a major draw."

One name had been conspicuously absent. Carter had no idea whether Felicity still planned to attend the reunion, but he guessed no. When he'd met her at SherryLee's shop to tell her that he was glad to see her but he wasn't interested in seeing her, she'd taken the news calmly, but he knew her well enough to know she'd been surprised. And disappointed.

Carter wondered whether she'd be as disappointed if she knew that the best years of his career were behind him. Wondered whether part of the reason she'd even considered reconciling with her high school boyfriend was because of his pro-athlete status.

Then there was Olive, who didn't care in the least that he was famous. Who would probably prefer it if he weren't.

Carter leaned forward and held out his casted hand, waiting with an expectant look as she tentatively placed her hand on the exposed part of his fingers.

"Shouldn't you be wearing your sling?" she asked.

"Nah. I'll be officially done with it next week anyway, and the angle of it has started to make my shoulder hurt more." With his good hand, he flipped hers over, palm up, and used his thumb to massage the center of her palm.

"And then what?"

"I'm not sure, exactly. It'll depend on what they find at my next appointment."

But he didn't want to think about that. Or the long year ahead of him dedicated to recovery. A year in which he'd be in the city, and Olive would be . . . here.

"So, what's next on this reunion business?" he asked, changing the subject.

"Easy stuff," Olive said. "I just need to make a few phone calls to secure the red carpet rental. Try to figure out if I can find a champagne fountain in our budget. Hire some kids from the theater department to dress up as paparazzi."

"Taking this 'Before They Were Famous' theme to the max, huh?"

She smiled distractedly, pulling her hand back and taking a sip of her water. "It's as close as most of us will get."

"Lucky dogs," he said with a wink.

She gazed at him over her water glass, then set it aside. "Did you like it? At the beginning?"

"What?"

"Being famous."

He was a little startled at the wording of her question. "Who says I don't like it now?"

"Do you?"

He thought it over. "I don't mind the being-famous part. It's the fact that nobody seems to want to see beneath the fame that gets to me."

"I've seen beneath it," she said, continuing to gaze steadily.

Carter felt something strange in his chest. "I know."

She waited a beat. "It's terrible."

Carter burst out laughing, relishing how this woman could make him feel things he'd never felt before and make him laugh like he'd never laughed before, all within the span of ten seconds.

"All right, so what can I do to help?"

"Nothing," she said, standing and picking up the pizza box, carrying it to the fridge. "In fact, it's probably a good idea if you back off entirely."

"What do you mean?" he asked, watching as she shoved the oversize box into the fridge with impressive force.

"Well, half the town already thinks something is brewing between us," she said, still jamming the box onto the shelf. "And I'm a terrible actor. If they see us together, they'll know in an instant that we sexed."

"Sexed? You've been spending too much time in the science classroom, and not enough in English class. You can't turn *sex* into a verb."

"I'm a biology teacher, which is all about sex, so I can do whatever I want," she said, lifting her fist in triumph when the pizza box finally caved to her will and she could close the door.

"Fine, call it whatever you want, so long as we can keep doing it."

She gave him a sultry smile that looked both nothing like Olive and exactly like Olive as she walked back toward him. "We can do it again—lots of agains—*if*," she said, lifting one leg to drop over his lap before lowering herself to straddle him, "we keep it a secret."

Carter was so distracted by the lush, right feel of her body on his that he nearly missed her words.

He reached around and wrapped his fingers gently around her ponytail, pulling the long blonde hair over her shoulder and inspecting the silky strands as he processed her words. "You want to keep it on the DL?"

"You disagree?" she asked, setting her fingers against his jaw and tracing her nails over his five-o'clock shadow, as though learning his shape.

"It's . . . new," he admitted.

She smiled. "Let me guess. Most women want to advertise they're sleeping with the Man of the Year?"

Carter winced. He'd forgotten that he had only another week until the magazine hit newsstands, trying to think about it as little as possible. Not because the title itself was so bad, or the story unearthed some big secret, but because he couldn't shake the sense that when it came out, everything would change. *This* would change.

"Don't worry," she said, giving him an affectionate pat. "I promise you're still the most impressive notch on my bedpost."

"Then why the secrecy?" he pressed, trying not to be irked that she was apparently embarrassed by their relationship.

She sighed and let her hand drop, then pulled back until her ponytail slipped from his fingers. Her expression turned serious. "It's not that I'm ashamed. And I'm not embarrassed," she said, reading his mind. "It's just . . ." Olive looked down, gathering her thoughts, before meeting his eyes once more. "In a week or so, this will all be over. You'll be back in the city, I'll be back at school. Who knows when we'll even see each other again, and when we do, there's a good chance we'll both be married. Me, probably to a fellow teacher, who has a hairpiece but is sweet to me. You, to a model, who also has a hairpiece in the form of extensions, who's sweet to you. I'm fine with that future. But in the meantime, I don't want to be *that* woman."

"What woman?" he asked, trying to ignore how much the picture she'd just painted bothered him.

"The one Carter Ramsey left behind," she said with a smile that didn't get anywhere near her eyes.

Carter's heart seemed to freeze in his chest, followed by a sharp sinking feeling in his stomach. "Olive."

"No. No. No." She lifted her hand and placed three fingers against his lips, silencing him. "Don't misunderstand. *I* won't think of myself as the woman you left behind. I neither want you to stay, nor do I want to go with you, and I can't think of a situation less suited to long distance than ours. But I can't stomach *other* people thinking that."

"I never pegged you as someone who cared about what others thought," he said, his words slightly muffled against her fingers.

She gave another of those tight smiles. "I've worked hard not to be. Most of us eccentrics learn early on our role in society, especially in a small town. You can either let it define you, or you can lean all the way into it. I've done the latter. But I've also worked hard to establish the Olive Dunn brand. Being associated with you will undo all of that. I'll cease to be the idiosyncratic but lovable high school teacher and become the *other* Haven girl that Carter Ramsey left behind."

"Ah," Carter said, understanding Olive a little more clearly now than he ever had. It wasn't that she'd built walls, per se. She was as open a person as he'd ever known, she knew who she was, and she genuinely liked who she was. But much of Olive's sense of security came from being the person who defined who she was. *She* let people know who Olive Dunn was, not the other way around. In many ways, it was the complete opposite of his life, where there was nonstop speculation on whom he was dating, how he was feeling, what he was thinking.

One more reason the two of them were incompatible in the long term.

"Are you disappointed that I won't be making a marriage pact with you?" she teased.

"Well, of course not," he said, smiling, because she expected him to. "How could you when you've got lofty plans to marry that nerdy teacher?"

"Exactly." She patted his chest. "Also, that pact was idiotic."

It was. He'd known it then, and he definitely knew it now.

And yet, there was apparently still a stupid eighteen-year-old boy inside him, because he desperately wanted to make Olive promise . . . something.

But Olive didn't belong in his life. He didn't have a normal nine-to-five schedule. He traveled more often than he was home, and when he was home, it had to be in the city.

Olive belonged here.

Even if he used his considerable resources to come see her in Haven as often as he could, after his injury healed, the best they could manage would be a few hours here and there between games and travel.

"So we're agreed?" Olive asked softly. "What happens between us stays between us?"

"Depends," Carter said with a wicked grin, running his hands over her thighs. "Can we be done with the reunion stuff for the night? I've got some other, more interesting things in mind."

She smiled against his mouth. "I like interesting."

Carter smiled back, even as his chest ached. *I like* you.

Chapter Twenty-Three

Nearly a month ago, Carter had stood in his penthouse kitchen and debated which was worse: the injury, or the fact that he'd been named Man of the Year.

He didn't know if it was ironic or fitting that the very day he had his cast removed was the day the magazine hit newsstands. He knew only that his phone had been buzzing all day with congratulations from friends and gentle ribs from teammates, and that . . . he didn't mind in the least.

The cast was off.

And he had someone to celebrate with.

Over the course of his career, Carter had developed a system for whenever he had something to celebrate. Depending on how big the win, how lucrative the contract, how highly regarded the accolade, he rewarded himself accordingly.

Outrageously expensive champagne after being named Rookie of the Year, even though he had barely been of legal age to drink and didn't particularly like champagne. A trip to Vegas to celebrate signing one of the largest contracts in MLB history, even though he didn't particularly like to gamble. A brand-new Porsche after winning his first AL MVP, even though he rarely had need for a car.

This time, he wanted to celebrate, and he had no use for Vegas, champagne, or a fancy new car.

He didn't want anything money could buy.

This time, the reward was the woman.

Carter didn't even bother going to the rental house. He saw Olive's car in her driveway and pulled Jody in right behind hers, bounding up the stairs before realizing he'd forgotten the beer, deciding, *Screw the beer*, and barging through her front door. He was thoroughly unsurprised to find it unlocked.

"Olive. You left your front door unlocked, again!" he called.

Her voice came from upstairs. "And yet strangely, I lived here for years without men barging in uninvited. Or coming by at all, really."

"Their loss," he said, about to go up the stairs toward her, but she was already coming down.

He couldn't hide his grin, and she matched it when she saw his left arm, launching herself at him much the way she had that day at the softball game.

This time, he caught her with both arms.

This time, he had no intention of letting her go.

"The cast is off," she said, leaning back just enough to clasp his face and sprinkle happy kisses all over him. "Feel good?" she asked.

"You have no idea," he said, still grinning at her, because *damn*— nobody ever made him smile as much as this woman. "I thought it would be bittersweet, knowing that it's only one part of the healing process, that the shoulder's still a mess, but I feel one step closer to whole. More like myself."

"Good," she said matter-of-factly, giving him one more kiss before squirming to be let go.

He held fast.

"Put me down. I want to show you something."

Reluctantly, he let her slide to the ground, and the second her feet hit the floor, she grabbed his hand and hauled him after her into the kitchen.

She gestured to the arrangement on her kitchen counter. "I didn't know if you were going to be in a champagne mood, a beer mood, a whisky mood, an iced-tea mood—"

"No on that last one."

"So I got them all," she said. "Because we have two things to celebrate: the liberation of your left arm, and"—she reached for something on the counter and turned around—"ta-da!"

He let out a laughing groan. "Are you trying to ruin my day?"

She smoothed a hand over the cover and gave it a fond pat. "I'm thinking of framing it."

"You will do no such thing."

"Why not? The rest of the town is."

Carter stared at her, horrified. "Please tell me you're joking."

Olive shook her head. "Not even a little bit. Your brilliant mother even anticipated it, and gave Gail over at Prints & More a heads-up to stock a bunch of 8.5 x 11 frames by today. I called to reserve one, but she's already out of stock."

"Oh God. Why? So they can preserve the memory and torture me later?"

Olive set the magazine aside and stepped closer, cupping his face. "Hardly. Haven is proud of you, Carter. They're proud of what you've accomplished. You might be *Citizen*'s man this year, but you've *always* been Haven's guy and always will be. I know you think the magazine didn't shed any light on who you are off the field, but we in Haven don't care. We don't even notice. Because we already know who you are off the field."

Carter took a deep breath, letting himself absorb everything she was saying, letting it ease some of the uncertainty and emptiness that he'd been carrying around for weeks. Months. Maybe years.

An emptiness that filled a little more with every day he was back in Haven, with every minute he was with her.

Olive kissed him softly. "I *like* that the magazine only shows the Baseball Carter. It means that the private side of you, the non-baseball Carter, is reserved for us lucky ones who know you personally. And we like getting a side of you that nobody else knows. A side that I happen to like very much."

He rested his forehead on hers. "*God*, I wish I'd found you in high school."

"Nah," she said, giving his chest a little pat. "We weren't ready for each other yet. Teenage Olive and Carter were pretty great, but Adult Olive and Carter are *really* great."

"Really great *together*," Carter corrected, pulling her closer.

She smiled. "It has been one hell of a summer fling."

Something in his chest tightened at her words, but Carter wasn't in the mood right now for regrets or might-have-beens.

He was in the mood for Olive.

His head lowered slowly, his lips capturing hers in a slow, breath-stealing kiss. Her response was immediate and eager, and when their lips finally pulled apart, both short for air, she reached down, linked their fingers, and wordlessly led him upstairs.

Since their first time together, he and Olive had slept together at least once a night, sometimes during the day, always when they were sure nobody would know.

Today was different. He made sure of it. Made sure that when he removed her shirt and bra, he showed her with lips and hands that her breasts were the most perfect he'd ever seen. When he tugged off her jeans, he let her know her toned legs were the sexiest, strongest he'd ever had the pleasure of touching. When he added her underwear to the ever-growing pile of clothes on the floor and parted her thighs and tasted her, he told her with his mouth that he was hers, as long as she'd have him.

And when Carter plunged inside her and felt he'd die from the pleasure, he told her and himself that she was his—only his—until it was time to go.

"Well," Olive said, long moments later, still panting as she rolled toward him and propped her elbows on his chest, her chin on her hands, looking up at him. "That was . . . epic."

He grinned up at the ceiling, wrapping his arm around her and idly playing with her hair. "I'll take *epic*. And if I may say so, I've had some pretty extravagant celebrations of good news in my day, but nothing has come close to what we just did."

Carter was joking as he said it, but the moment the words were out, he felt the truth of them and realized that the intimacy he and Olive had just experienced hadn't just been about communicating something to her—he'd been discovering something about himself: these past few weeks with this woman had brought out the very best in him. They were the best of him.

"Okay, for real," she said, rubbing her palm over his chest hair, watching the motion instead of looking at him. "What happens next for you?"

"After the surgery, you mean?" He exhaled. "Rest. Recovery. A whole lot of PT. Worst case, I'll start throwing baseballs backwards through kitchen windows, like a certain woman I once knew, and my career's officially over."

She pinched his side. "What's best case?"

"Best case, they'll have to replace my Man of the Year title with Miracle Man, and I'll be back in the majors as good as ever, with a World Series ring to prove it."

"Miracle Man," she mused. "For the record, I will not be calling you that."

"No?" He shifted so that he could roll on his side, facing her. "What will you call me after I'm gone?"

"Baseball," she said definitively, referring to her initial nickname for him.

"And after I no longer play baseball?" he said, tucking a strand of blonde hair behind her ear, letting his fingers linger there.

"Well, I've been thinking about that." She stacked her hands beneath her cheek. "I know I said you were more than baseball, and you are. So much more. But I also think it's a part of you that won't ever go away."

"I see. You picture me rounding the bases in a wheelchair in my eighties?"

"No." She smiled. "I think that when your playing days are over, whether it's at the end of this contract, or if you play another twenty years, the league will refuse to let you go. You'll be a coach, or a manager. And when you're too old for that, maybe you could be a cute old man on TV or radio barking about what happens."

"An announcer?"

"Yes!" she said, sounding pleased with her scenario.

Too pleased for his liking, considering the closest she'd be to that would be on the watching or listening side right here in Haven with her husband with the hairpiece.

"Will you watch?" he couldn't stop himself from asking.

"Watch what?"

"My games. The ones that I play, when I'm back. The ones that I coach. The ones I announce."

"Mmm." She pressed her lips together and avoided his gaze as she thought it over. "Not at first. I think it might be a little raw."

"Yeah?" He slid his palm against hers, their hands clasped in the space between them. He was both pleased to know she wouldn't be unscathed when he left and bothered by the thought of her hurting.

"Yeah. Turns out I like you a little bit," she said softly, with a faint smile. "But," she said, recovering her assertive Olive tone immediately, "I'll snap back so quickly they'll start calling me the Miracle Woman."

"Except they won't. Because nobody knows we've seen each other naked and have pillow talk at two p.m. on a weekday."

"Oh right. That reminds me, do you have one of your baseball outfits? Or can you get one by the reunion on Saturday?"

"My outfits?"

"Costume?" she said sweetly.

His eyes narrowed. "You're messing with me."

"Very good." She patted his cheek. "For the reunion, everyone's supposed to dress up as what they'd be if they were famous. For you, there's no if. Ergo—suit up, Man of the Year."

"Fine. What will you be going as? What are you famous for, in this high school reunion fantasy land?"

She smiled and leaned in for a kiss. "Guess you'll just have to show up on Saturday to find out."

Chapter Twenty-Four

Saturday, September 5

Because Carter knew way more about the nuances of high school reunions after these past few weeks than he'd ever thought he would, he knew that the average Haven High reunion attendance was about 30 percent.

But when Olive Dunn was behind it? A whopping 81 percent of their graduating class RSVPed yes.

And from the near-roar of the packed gymnasium, it seemed just about every last one of the yeses had shown up.

Everyone except Felicity, who'd slipped out of town as quietly as she'd come in, which confirmed the town's suspicions that she'd come back solely with hopes of winning the heart of her former prom king, only to ditch out when she realized he was taken.

And he was very much taken.

Speaking of which, where *was* Olive?

Had her mysterious costume disguised her so thoroughly, he was failing to find her among the sea of classmates and their plus-ones?

No. That wasn't it. Carter was certain he could pick Olive Dunn out of any crowd. Now. Forever.

Except they didn't have forever. They had even less time than they'd thought, which was why he really needed her here—so he could tell her.

"So, small bone to pick with you," Adam Santiago said, clinking his beer to Carter's, and jolting Carter back to the conversation at hand. "I'm out fifty bucks, and it's your fault."

"How's that?" Carter asked amicably, figuring Adam had bet on some baseball game and lost.

"There was a pool going on whether or not you'd be here with Felicity George tonight. I thought for sure you were going to hit that, man."

"Dude." One of Adam's more sober friends elbowed him hard. "Shut up."

Carter looked at the less drunk of the two, pinning him with a gaze. "Explain."

Elliott gave a nervous shrug. "Just some stupid wager that started a few weeks back. There was a rumor going around that you were in town to get back together with her. Everyone knows you were a hot item back . . . before."

"Yeah, before Olive," said Britney Cors teasingly, a girl he'd had a thirty-second relationship with their freshman year, who was now happily married with four kids.

"Wait, what?" Adam asked, clearly tipsy and slow to keep up with the conversation. "Olive Dunn?"

"How many Olives are there?" Britney said in exasperation.

"Damn. How'd I miss that?"

"Because you're an idiot," Britney's husband muttered under his breath.

Carter nearly spoke up to say that he and Olive were just friends. It was what she wanted—not to be known as the woman he left behind—but the words wouldn't come. He didn't want a single person here to think he was ashamed of being romantically entangled with Olive.

"Well, that's cool," an oblivious Adam said. "Olive's the best."

Carter narrowed his eyes on the shorter man, looking for any sign of sarcasm, because though he thoroughly agreed with the assessment, he also remembered high school. People hadn't been cruel to Olive, but they hadn't been particularly kind, either.

Brian Nickles, the first basemen to Carter's shortstop back in high school, smiled and nodded in agreement with Adam. "Olive's baller. She reminds me of a Valkyrie."

"She's a gosh-darn doll," said Brian's wife in a slight southern twang. Carter'd forgotten her name, but remembered she was from Alabama.

Again, Carter looked for sarcasm, ready to fight for Olive's honor, and again he saw only honest nods.

"Everyone likes Olive," Alabama continued. "If there were a homecoming queen for grown-ups, she'd be it." She looked around at the group. "*Was* she homecoming queen in high school?"

"Nah," Joe Bianchi said. "We were too dumb and stupid to see the good ones back then," he added, echoing thoughts very similar to ones Carter himself had been having in recent weeks.

"Hey!" his pregnant wife said, poking her finger into his stomach.

"Whoops. Forgot I married my high school sweetheart," he said, bending to kiss her cheek.

"He's right, though," Courtney said to no one in particular. "I admit I wasn't all that nice to Olive in high school. She was smart, and smart wasn't cool, and well . . . that's kind of embarrassing to admit now, isn't it?"

"What's embarrassing?"

Carter's blood immediately seemed to run warmer as the group turned slightly to welcome the newcomer.

Olive . . . covered in green glitter.

"Oh my God," Courtney said, laughing so hard that she had to adjust her Wonder Woman tiara—her ideal version of famous, apparently. "What are you, the Jolly Green Giant?"

"No, she's Gumby!" someone else guessed. "Jesus, Olive, you're way too hot for your famous alter ego to be a creepy clay children's toy."

"Um, duh," Elliott said. "Which is why she's obviously Gamora. The hot chick from *Guardians of the Galaxy*."

Noting the other man's admiring tone, Carter gave Elliott a sharp look. Elliott was divorced, and not unattractive. He was also dressed up as Chris Pratt's character from *Guardians of the Galaxy*, giving him and Olive a decidedly couple-y vibe.

For that matter, Marvel and DC Comics apparently played an important role in most of Haven High School's graduates' version of *famous*. That or, more likely, they'd all used the night as a chance to dress up as whatever they had been at Halloween.

"Wrong, wrong, and wrong," Olive said playfully, pointing at each of the incorrect guesses. She looked every bit the queen holding court, and had still not once looked Carter's way.

Nobody was looking Carter's way.

So much for Man of the Year being the draw tonight. These people had shown up because Olive had asked them to.

Carter smiled at the realization. It was exactly as it should be.

"Okay, so who are you, for real?" someone asked.

"I," Olive said, dramatically, as she put her hand to her chest, "am a high school biology teacher, who in the process of trying to make posters for her high school reunion, managed to cover herself in green glitter."

This earned her a few quizzical smiles. But Carter understood.

"You're yourself," Carter said to her, speaking for the first time.

Olive's blue eyes cut to his, and she smiled at him, friendly and guileless. "I'm me. And me is better than famous."

"If you don't put that quote on Pinterest, I will," said a woman dressed in an astronaut costume.

"Go for it," Olive said. "Pinterest and all its lofty ideals is what got me into this glitter mess in the first place."

"Ohmigod," another of their classmates said, all but bouncing as the DJ started playing a slow song. "I *love* this song. You guys remember it? It was the last slow dance they played at prom."

Olive gave an indifferent shrug. "I didn't go to prom."

Carter looked at her in dismayed surprise. *Well.* That was some bullshit.

Screw her secrecy plan. Carter knew what he had to do. What he wanted to do. Especially since their time was more limited than she realized. He wasn't waiting another moment.

He set his drink on a table and stepped forward, hand extended to the most dazzling woman he'd ever known, with or without glitter. "Dance with me, Dunn."

She took his hand and smiled back, and Carter felt his heart crack a little knowing what he needed to tell her tonight.

That tonight was their *last* night.

Chapter Twenty-Five

Saturday, September 5

"Well. This isn't going to help quell the rumors that we're hooking up," Olive said, even as she rested her head on his shoulder, feeling as much at home as she ever had.

"I hardly think that's our biggest problem," Carter said against her hair, his cheek resting on the top of her head.

"What's worse in your mind? That my costume is better than your costume?" she asked.

"How about the fact that your costume is getting green glitter all over my uniform? Can't wait to explain *that* when I hand it over to be dry-cleaned."

She smiled, because while his tone was all cranky superstar, his arm slid farther around her waist, pulling her even closer.

Olive knew that rumors would be swirling nonstop about her and Carter after tonight, but she no longer cared. It didn't matter that people would talk. It didn't matter that after he left, everyone would know he'd also left her.

Olive cared only that she and Carter made the most of these last couple of weeks they had left.

"You might have warned me, you know," Carter said.

"About what?"

"That I'd been dethroned as our graduating class's golden boy. As far as I can tell, you're the golden *girl*."

She said nothing for a moment as they swayed, thinking it over. "I don't know if it's that so much. Maybe just that I'm *here*."

Carter looked away without saying anything, and her stomach sank at the realization of how her comment had sounded.

"Carter, I didn't mean—"

"No, it's fine," he said stiffly. "You're absolutely right. You stayed. You thrived. I can't imagine Haven without you."

"I—I don't know that I'd say *thrive*, but . . ." She took a deep breath. "I have to say, I can't wait for school to start on Tuesday. I feel like a kid before Christmas."

He pulled back enough to meet her eyes, arms still locked around her waist, high school–dance style. "Yeah? You haven't talked about it much."

"No." She gave a slight smile. "Partially because it's pretty second nature for me now. I feel good about the curriculum I've developed, and it's not like elementary school, where you have to decorate the classroom to be friendly. But I guess I haven't really talked about it because the start of the school year also coincides with—"

"Me leaving," he finished for her.

She met his eyes with a sad smile, and their gazes locked and held for a long, meaningful stretch. The bittersweetness of the moment almost took her breath away: two people who cared about each other enough to want the best for the other, even as it would drive them apart.

As though he'd heard her thoughts, Carter's smile dimmed slightly, and he blew out a breath. "Olive, I need to tell you something."

"Now?" she asked, the song coming to an end, replaced by some throwback dance hit she knew all the words to, but wouldn't be able to name either in title or artist if her life depended on it.

"It can wait," he hedged.

"No, no, it'll just fester," she said impatiently, grabbing his hand and dragging him out a side door of the gym, no longer caring that at least a dozen pairs of eyes tracked their movement.

The night was warm and muggy, just as the gym had been, and Olive delicately swiped at a trickle of sweat running a sparkly green river along her temple. "What's up?"

"My manager called me this afternoon," Carter said.

"And?"

He squeezed his eyes shut, just for a moment, looking tormented, before opening them and meeting her gaze with a tortured expression. "They want to reschedule the surgery."

"Well. Yeah," she said, puzzled. "Not exactly a news flash."

He crossed his arms and looked down at his feet, then back at her. "They moved it up a couple weeks. It's scheduled for Tuesday morning."

"*This* Tuesday?" she repeated, pleased that her voice didn't break, even though it was higher than she was used to hearing.

"I'm sorry. I didn't know until today. I didn't—"

Her mind reeled, but she held up a hand. "No, Carter. Please. Don't apologize. It's fine. We've known it's coming. What difference does a week or two make?"

He flinched as though she'd hurt him. "A lot, I'd say, when a week or two was all we had left."

And whose fault is that? The thought ripped through her, pernicious and unfair, but intense and unavoidable.

Carter was leaving. This thing between them, whatever it was, would go with him. And it wasn't coming back.

She prided herself on being a smart, reasonable woman. She knew that even if he came back for Thanksgiving or Christmas, or even for a week in his off-season, it wouldn't be the same. They could have fling after fling, but that's all it would ever be. It would never recapture the magic of this summer, where, for one tiny stretch of her life, everything had been . . . perfect.

He'd pushed her buttons, made her crazy, pissed her off. He'd been her challenger, her friend, her lover, her . . . everything. And he was leaving.

Tomorrow.

She stepped forward, right hand extended.

He stared down at her hand. "You have got to be kidding me."

Olive scowled. "Don't be unsportsmanlike. Shake my hand. It's rude not to."

"Oh, it's *rude*?" he mocked. "You know what's rude, Olive? Ending a pretty damn great affair with a handshake."

"You know what's even more rude?" she said, continuing the immature pattern, her voice colder now. "Telling a woman to her face that she was an *affair*."

"How is that any different than you calling it a fling? And what do you want me to call it, Olive?" he said, practically shouting. "You don't want to come with me!"

"And you don't want to stay!" she yelled back, completely uncaring whether anyone heard them.

His jaw worked. "I can't stay. You know that."

She did know that.

Olive crossed her arms. "And I can't go. You know that."

He squeezed his eyes shut, his head tipping back in frustration. "Jesus."

Her eyes watered, and she realized in irritation that for the second time in a week this man was about to make her cry. She didn't want that. She didn't want any of this hurt. But it was here, and she had to deal with it.

The best she could do for both of them was to end it as quickly as possible. There was a reason everyone knew ripping the Band-Aid off was the best approach. She'd also learned a few things growing up with a workaholic single dad and not much in the way of friends: you had to do the hard stuff yourself.

"I'm really happy for you, Carter—I mean, not that you have to have surgery, but that it's the start of getting you back to where you want to be: the baseball field." He opened his mouth, but she held up her hand. "Wait, let me finish. I'm happy for you, and your dreams. I know you're happy for me, and mine. But they're not compatible. We both know that. We've both known that. It's better for both of us if we just . . . call it."

Carter didn't say anything or move for a long moment. Then finally, he nodded, the gesture jerky.

She managed a jerky nod of her own before turning to return to the gym, not entirely sure how she was supposed to force a happy face for the rest of the night but determined to try.

Carter grabbed her hand. "Olive. Wait."

Her breath caught, and she turned back around.

"I've got to go," he whispered, his eyes looking suspiciously shiny. "But know that I'll always . . . My time here in Haven, with you, it's been . . ." He blew out a frustrated breath. "Olive, I think I—"

"Don't, Carter," she whispered, feeling the tears threaten to create white stripes down her green-glitter face. "Don't."

Chapter Twenty-Six

Sunday, September 6

"Oh God. You must have looked *awful*."

Kelly gave Caitlyn an exasperated look as she handed Olive a martini across the bed. "Yes, Cait, that's *definitely* the most important part of the story."

"I'm just saying, she covered herself in green glitter, got sweaty, and cried. It couldn't have been pretty," Caitlyn said sympathetically, patting Olive's hand.

Caitlyn, grumpy over having had to miss the reunion because of her continued bed rest, had insisted on a girls' night to rehash the evening. Needless to say, she and Kelly had gotten more than they'd bargained for when Olive had told them about her and Carter's implosion.

"It *wasn't* pretty," Olive said, pulling the toothpick out of her martini and sliding an olive off with her teeth, munching despondently. "And it didn't help that as chair, I had to put on a happy face the rest of the evening."

"I don't think you were all that successful," Caitlyn said with a grimace as she pulled a cracker off the cheese tray. "Obviously nobody knew exactly what went down between you two, but everybody knows something did. The group text messages this morning were *intense*."

"Caitlyn!" Kelly said, exasperated. "How is this helpful?"

"It's fine," Olive said with a tired sigh, courtesy of a really sore heart and a sleepless night. "She's not saying anything that's not true."

Caitlyn squeezed her hand. "For what it's worth, if I have to take sides, I'd take yours. At the moment, I'd much rather claim you as my sister instead of that stupid pighead brother I shared the womb with."

"I appreciate it," Olive said. "But it's not like we actually thought this was going to end any differently. Did we?" She looked between the two of them.

"No," Kelly admitted with a sigh, dropping down in the chair opposite Olive on the other side of Caitlyn's bed, pulling her hair into a messy bun. "But I think I speak for the entire freaking town when I say we were really hoping for something different."

Olive snorted. "What, that I'd become a baseball girlfriend? Start wearing hats on the third baseline?"

"Girlfriends more commonly sit on the first-base side. Or behind home plate," Caitlyn said.

"See, exactly the type of thing Carter Ramsey's ideal wife would know," Olive said, making a double-decker sandwich out of the cheddar and Ritz crackers from the cheese plate on Caitlyn's nightstand. "And exactly the kind of thing I don't."

"Whoa," Kelly said.

"What?"

"You said *wife*," Kelly said. "That's an interesting step up from *girlfriend*."

"I was just making a point," Olive said, spraying crumbs.

"Okay, sweetie, let's limit to no more than three pieces of cheese going into your mouth at the same time. Men aren't worth losing all our dignity."

"Oh yeah?" Olive said to Kelly, her words still muffled by the monster stack of cheese and crackers she'd stuffed into her mouth. "So you really kept it together when you and Mark were fumbling your way through love, huh?"

"Mark and I have nothing to do with you and—wait, *love?*" Kelly shot an alarmed look over Olive's shoulder to Caitlyn. "*Wife* and *love*. Are you hearing this?"

"I am," Caitlyn said, looking both intrigued and worried. "Is that what this is, Liv? You love him?"

"I don't know," Olive said with a sigh, washing down the cheese and crackers with a sip of the Grey Goose dirty martini Kelly had made. "What does that even feel like?"

Neither said anything for a long minute. Finally, Caitlyn took a stab at it. "It can feel like a lot of things. Like you can't breathe when you're with the person. Like you can *only* breathe with the person . . ."

"Or like they make you really crazy, but you'll also go crazy if you're not with him," Kelly chimed in.

Olive bit her lip, because both of those descriptions exactly described how she felt about Carter Ramsey.

"Oh, hun," Kelly said, apparently reading Olive's expression. "I have to ask, if you even *suspected* it might be love, why did you—"

"I *had* to let him go," Olive said. "Even if he'd wanted to stay, and he did not, he has two years left on a bazillion-dollar contract."

"Okay, just tell me to back off if I'm pushing too hard, because I know I do that, but did you ever *ask* Carter to stay?" Caitlyn said. "I mean not to quit his contract, but to make it work somehow? Would it have been possible for you to stay here in Haven, but you somehow still be together?"

Olive stared glumly at her martini, not really wanting it. Not wanting *anything*. Cheese hadn't helped. The ice cream she'd had for breakfast hadn't helped. It didn't matter how many dirty martinis Kelly made, she only felt . . . numb.

"No," Olive answered finally. "I didn't ask him. What would be the point?"

"Did he ever ask you to join him?" Kelly asked curiously.

Olive flinched. "No. He did not."

"Did you want him to?" Caitlyn asked.

She continued to stare blindly into her drink. Stabbing at the bobbing olives, without really seeing them. "My life is here."

A life that no longer felt full.

"What if he *had* asked?" Kelly pressed.

Olive shook her head. "He wouldn't. His career is everything to him."

"It *was* everything to him," Caitlyn said. "But from everything you've described, I have to think he's come to care about you, too."

"Maybe. But I care about him too much to ask him to give anything up for me."

"There," Kelly said very softly. *"That's* love."

Olive merely closed her eyes, unable to deny any longer than she was completely in love with Carter Ramsey. And equally unsure about what to do about it.

"I do love him, but I also love my life here. I'm not the girl who gives it all up for some boy," she whispered. *"I won't* be that girl."

Neither of her friends had a solution for that. Because there wasn't one.

Chapter Twenty-Seven

Monday, September 7

Most people in Haven spent Labor Day at barbecues, celebrating the last honorary day of summer before the start of the school year.

Olive appreciated that she was always invited to several, but she always declined. She had a beloved holiday tradition of her own. One that involved fluorescent lights, arranging lab desks, and lining up the chalk just so—she liked to do things the old-fashioned way—so everything was exactly where she wanted it to be.

Olive loved the first day of school, but she loved the day before the first day of school even more. It was a chance to celebrate everything she loved about her life, her job, the fact that she'd set out to shape young minds, and was doing exactly that.

But today, as she let herself into the science wing, she didn't quite feel the usual spark. She hadn't felt anything even remotely *resembling* a spark since Saturday night, when she and Carter had parted ways.

She'd spent last night on Caitlyn and AJ's couch, not ready to face the prospect of going home to where Carter was so close physically, but a million miles away emotionally. She'd wanted to put off the moment where she'd have to go home and not see Carter's red truck in the driveway.

She frowned a little, wondering what he'd done with Jody. When he'd first arrived he'd said he was planning to sell it when he left to go back to the city. But then, she supposed plenty had changed between now and then. Maybe he'd decided to keep the truck.

The truck. But not the girl.

Swallowing anything resembling pointless regret, she shoved her key into her classroom door. She'd been in once or twice over the summer, but she'd meant it when she'd told Carter there wasn't much to do in the way of setup these days. She had her classroom as she liked it, and her Labor Day ritual was more a mental preparation for the school year than an actual necessary task.

The rest of the science wing was quiet as she opened the door to her classroom, most of the other teachers having done their setup last week, so that they could spend Labor Day with rosé and hot dogs in hand.

Olive was as familiar with the layout of her classroom as she was her own home, so she stepped into the room even before reaching for the light. Her shin rammed into something, and she let out a pained grunt, her hand fumbling for the light switch as she mentally cursed the idiot who had moved around furniture without her permission.

It wasn't furniture, she realized as the lights flickered on. It was a really big shipping box. One of several.

Puzzled, she set her bag on one of the student desks and checked the label. They were all addressed to her, with the school's address, but the return name was an acronym that told her nothing.

Using her keys as a box cutter, she opened the box she'd run into and was pretty sure would leave a bruise on her shin. Inside were four smaller cardboard boxes, equally unmarked. She pulled one out and carefully began opening it, the massive amounts of padding and Styrofoam telling her the contents were fragile or, at the very least, expensive.

A moment later, she tugged away the last bit of packaging and stared.

Fragile and expensive.

And very, very precious.

She let out an excited *whoop* that echoed through the empty classroom, the cell structure and periodic table of elements posters on the wall doing little to absorb the sound. Then, not wanting to get ahead of herself, she opened a second box, just to make sure it wasn't some sort of sick practical joke where they'd sent just the one, and the rest were empty.

By the fourth, she knew it was no joke.

Someone had sent her a whole lot of microscopes. And not just any microscopes, but top-of-the-line, shockingly expensive microscopes.

Frowning, she put her hands on her hips, wondering when Principal Mullins had changed his mind. Wondering where he'd gotten the money. Wondering why a man who'd once asked if she couldn't just give the students "some sort of complex plant coloring book" to help them understand photosynthesis would suddenly make such a huge financial investment in science.

Wondering, most of all, why her boss wouldn't have told her.

Mullins wasn't a bad man, and she believed that he really did mean well, even if she didn't agree with most of his approach to education. But he was also a little bit of a blowhard. The type of guy who would make sure you knew it was him if he did you a favor. There was no way he wouldn't find some way to take credit.

Olive carefully went through the boxes, unpacking each microscope carefully, but also inspecting each box for a note or receipt or indication of where they'd come from. On the outside of the final box, she found it.

Next to the shipping label was a plastic bag, the kind used to include shipping insurance documentation. There was that, as well as a receipt—the total took her breath away.

And stuffed behind the paperwork was one last folded set of papers, glossy, colored, and familiar: the cover of *Citizen* magazine, plus a few torn-out pages of the featured story.

Olive stared down at Carter's face, wistfully drawing a finger over his jawline beneath the Man of the Year text. Olive had never been one to collect posters and magazines of teen heartthrobs, but apparently she was a late bloomer.

The inclusion of the magazine told her what she'd already suspected—that Principal Mullins hadn't had anything to do with the microscopes. Probably hadn't even known about them.

They'd been a gift from a man whose heart and generosity were every bit as big as his bank account.

Still, she was a little hurt by the lack of a personal note.

She turned over the pages of the *Citizen* magazine story she'd already read several times, and paused when she got to the last page, where someone had scrawled notes in the margin:

Fast facts about the man beneath the uniform

Favorite wine: Zinfandel, especially shared with good neighbors

Favorite color: Green, particularly in glitter form

Favorite animal: Haven Lions

Favorite possession: Jody

Favorite school subject: Science. Because it's damned important. And because I met a girl there my senior year. I think I love her.

Olive read the words dozens of times. Maybe hundreds, before finally lifting her hands and swiping at her cheeks, realizing how wrong she'd been.

She belonged in Haven, yes. But she also belonged with Carter.

No way was she going to let him go without a fight.

Chapter Twenty-Eight

The doctors had warned him that despite it being a straightforward outpatient surgery, his shoulder would hurt after.

They were right.

But aside from the first pain pill he'd taken immediately after getting home that afternoon, he hadn't bothered to take any others. They didn't do much to numb the real pain.

The kind not in his left shoulder but just south and center of it.

The TV muted in the background, he reached for his phone again and found a few messages, most from his teammates, who'd finally been told of the extent of his injury. Four texts from his mother, even though he'd already talked to his parents three times since he'd gotten back from surgery. A *Dumb and Dumber* GIF from Caitlyn, because his twin knew they always made him laugh.

But nothing from the person he wanted to hear from the most.

He knew the microscopes had been delivered, because he'd gotten the delivery confirmation. Carter had been so damn sure it had been a baller move. Just about the only kind of grand gesture that could sweep a woman like Olive Dunn off her feet. In fact, he'd been so sure it would win her back, he'd added her name to his "approved guest" list in his building, thinking she might race into the city.

Nothing.

Not that he'd done it only for that reason. He'd have bought the microscopes regardless—had started researching the second she'd mentioned what an idiot her principal was. For that, he didn't need gratitude. It was just the right thing to do, and he'd wanted to do it.

The magazine, though—what he'd written in the magazine . . .

He'd stupidly gotten his hopes up that putting it all on the line might give him a chance.

Nope.

The baseball game came back from commercial, but he didn't bother to unmute it. He was still rooting for his team, but they were looking like a no-go for postseason, and for the first time in his life, he had something more important on his mind than baseball.

A month ago, Carter hadn't even known that was possible.

He gingerly got off the couch, careful not to jostle the arm, which was once again immobile in a splint. And this time, there'd be no Olive to help him when he got tangled.

Feeling aimless, he wandered around his apartment, looking at the bags he'd started to pack, at the couple of cardboard boxes he'd grabbed from the recycling room in his building because they looked to be in good enough condition for reuse.

Feeling foolish for bothering.

Feeling foolish for turning a summer fling into something it wasn't.

Carter absently tapped the corner of his phone against his kitchen counter. Maybe he was being ridiculous. This wasn't high school. He wasn't just a boy with a crush. He was a man who missed the woman he loved.

Just call her, you idiot.

He had started to when someone knocked at his door. Loud, impatient, and followed immediately by a rattling of the doorknob, then another impatient thump.

Carter instantly felt every ounce of tension leave his body—forgot, even, the pain in his shoulder. He knew only one person who had such utter disdain for locked doors.

Keeping his face neutral, he casually opened the door. "This isn't Haven, Dunn. People don't just lock their doors, they lock automatically."

"Well yeah, in fancy buildings like this one," she said, letting herself into his apartment. "It's like freaking Fort Knox down there. I had to show my ID, and I'm pretty sure he wanted to ask for my social security number and thumbprint."

"How'd you know where I lived?" he asked curiously, closing the door.

"I faked a rash, then sweet-talked your dermatologist dad into giving me the address."

He laughed, because it was so Olive. "What kind of rash?"

"Very intimate. You don't want to know," she said.

"How intimate?" he said in a low voice. "I might."

She smiled, but it was distracted as her gaze drifted over him, locking on the shoulder. "Back in your straitjacket, huh? How'd the surgery go?"

He shrugged his good shoulder. "Routine. The injury's relatively straightforward, as is the surgery. It's just the healing that's the bitch."

"I'm sorry. I wanted to be here, but—first day of school . . ."

"Right," he said, feeling suddenly foolish for resenting her silence. "How'd that go?"

"Pretty great, actually," Olive said with a grin. "See, I got these amazing, brand-new microscopes . . . Oh wait. You know about that, don't you?"

He smiled and shoved a hand into his jeans pocket. "Why would I know about that?"

"Uh-huh," she said, walking toward him. Her smile turned quieter as she stood in front of him. "Thank you," she said. "I can't even tell you how much it meant. I want to tell you that it was too much, that I can't accept it, but I am one hundred percent going to accept it, because it's for the kids—"

"And for you," he said softly. "The kids will benefit, and I'm glad for it, but I did it because someone with as much passion as you have for teaching deserves the best tools. You deserve a hell of a lot better resources than what your shortsighted principal is giving you."

"I do," she said, in typical Olive fashion. "Which reminds me, I should have said thank you last night, but I got kind of distracted . . ."

She tapped his chest once with her finger—*wait here*—then went to her purse and pulled out her cell phone, flipping through screens until she found what she wanted.

"I found this," Olive said, handing him the phone.

Carter took it, scrolled through the web page, then looked up. "Spell it out for the dumb jock."

She rolled her eyes at his self-deprecating humor, but answered him anyway. "Principal Mullins is entitled to his opinions, but it got me thinking. I have my opinions, too, and they're good ones. The kind of big-thinking opinions very well suited to leadership."

"You'll make an excellent president," he joked.

"Obviously. But I was thinking more along the lines of school principal. Principal Dunn has a damn fine ring to it, doesn't it?"

"Sure," he said, a little confused, but no less happy for her. "I think you'd be great—"

"The thing is, I need to get my master's in education administration to do that." She swallowed, her hands twisting slightly. "I'm applying to Columbia." She pointed at the college website on her phone, which he still held. "Even if I get in, I need to finish this school year and wouldn't start classes until fall of next year." She swallowed, seeming nervous for the first time since marching in his front door—since the first time ever. "But if I did get accepted, there's a very good chance I would need to live in New York City while I complete the program."

"Olive." He tentatively reached for her. "I can't let you—"

"I'm not Felicity," Olive interrupted gently. "I'm not telling you I'm skipping college to follow you around and be your groupie. I'm not an eighteen-year-old girl in puppy love looking to do whatever it takes to be near her boyfriend."

The hope that had just started to bloom in his chest crumbled to his feet, leaving nothing but a hollow, dead feeling.

She walked toward him with purpose, taking the phone out of his hand and flinging it onto his couch. She stood before him and met his eyes, unflinching. "What I am is a very smart woman who's figured out how to have the life I want with the man I want. And that man is you."

Carter's hand cupped her head as his mouth crashed over hers, too elated to be cool, too in love to wait a second longer.

Her arms went around his neck, strong and sure as she kissed him back as though they'd been separated for years instead of days.

He finally pulled back, touching her face gently. "But what about Haven High? I know how important the school and community are to you."

"It *is* extremely important to me, which is why I fully intend to make a glorious return. As principal."

"When's that?"

"My degree will take two years," she said, tracing a finger gently over his collarbone. "And correct me if I'm wrong, but your contract is up around that same time. Though if you plan to re-sign—"

"I want to play baseball again, Olive. I want to finish what I started," he interrupted gently. "But I don't want to play baseball forever."

"Even if you did, I'd be right there with you. If anyone can do long distance, it's us."

Carter felt a suspicious prick behind his eyes, realizing he'd found the woman—the one who loved him regardless of his baseball skill, and also in spite of it.

Olive started looking around his apartment, a slight frown on her face. "What are all these boxes for? Are you moving?"

"Let's just say I'd been rethinking my rehab plan. Was thinking of maybe making Haven my home base, and commuting into the city as necessary."

She looked up, stunned. "You planned that before you knew I was coming here today?"

He touched her cheek. "Not so much planned as hoped."

"But wherever will you live?" she asked playfully.

"Well, I know a house I could rent, though where I really want to be is shacked up with the girl next door."

Olive brushed her lips over his. "I'm pretty sure we can figure something out. We'll figure all of it out."

"Damn straight, future Principal Dunn."

"Oh, about that," she said, leaning into him, and pressing her lips just beneath his ear. "I was sort of thinking that someday in the distant future I might be Principal *Ramsey* . . ."

"Someday," Carter agreed, pulling her closer. "But there'll be nothing *distant* about it."

Epilogue

"Eyes on the ball, Torrie!"

Olive grinned and took a sip of her hot chocolate. She'd heard that one before.

It was unusually cold for early October, but nobody cared, least of all the dozen or so six-year-old girls getting their first taste of softball.

One of them had been playing since she was in diapers.

Olive shifted on the cold bleacher, her gaze seeking and finding the tallest person on the field by several feet. Carter Ramsey, coach of Haven High's all-state baseball team and the Haven first-grade softball team.

Not yet a championship-level team, but Carter had big plans.

"Melissa! Jolie! Girls, what did we say about cartwheels in the outfield when someone is up to bat?" Carter called.

Olive lifted her fingers to her lips to cover the smile, but not before she felt his gaze boring into her profile. She darted her gaze toward home plate and, sure enough, found her husband of seven years giving her a mock glare.

"Girls," Carter called, without looking away from Olive, "take a five-minute break to play catch with your assigned buddy. And remember, do not pick the dead flowers."

Carter never took his eyes off her as he made his way toward her, losing the battle with his fake glare the closer he got, until his eyes glowed warm, and he bent down, placing a soft kiss on her mouth. "Thought you had to work late, Principal Ramsey."

"Turns out some things are more important than work," she said, lifting her face to his for a more proper greeting.

"Eww, gross." A tall girl with a long ponytail marched over toward them, a brown-looking weed clenched in her hand.

Carter closed his eyes and sighed. "Torrie. What did I say about the flowers?"

"*Taraxacum officinale* is more of a weed. Right, Mom?"

"Quite right," Olive said. "Though when your dad says not to pick the flowers, I think he includes dandelions in that."

Torrie nodded dutifully, then gasped as she looked down at her forearm. "Look! A ladybug." She gave Carter a beseeching look. "You said we needed a team name. If this isn't a sign, I don't know what is."

With that, she raced off toward her friends in a gangly lope.

Carter shook his head. "Your daughter."

"*Our* daughter."

"Indeed. Did I tell you said daughter asked if she could take my World Series ring in for show-and-tell on Friday?" Carter asked.

"Which one? You can just tell her they're too valuable, she'll understand."

"Nah," he said, smiling, as he leaned down for another kiss. "Those aren't the most valuable things in my life." He reached for her left hand, rubbing his thumb over the gloriously, embarrassingly large diamond ring. "One." He turned and looked across the field to where Torrie was dangling a worm at her best friend. "Two."

Carter turned back to Olive and pressed another soft kiss to her mouth that lingered just a little bit hot for a first-grade softball practice, and she slowly took his hand and pressed it to her not-yet-showing belly and whispered the news she'd been dying to tell him since her doctor's appointment that afternoon. "Three."

AUTHOR'S NOTE

Dear reader,

Thank you so much for taking time out of your busy life to read *Yours to Keep*. Olive and Carter's story was particularly fun to write, and you're probably thinking, "Oh, she says that with every book." I assure you, I do not. While I love the finished product of all my books equally, some stories have that little extra *something* during the writing process, where my fingers fly over the keyboard, where I find myself smiling long after I've shut the laptop for the day. *Yours to Keep* is one of those stories.

If you enjoyed reading it even half as much as I enjoyed writing it, I hope you'll check out my backlist, especially *Yours in Scandal*, featuring the first of "my guys" to be named Man of the Year (the hot young NYC mayor who's mentioned a couple of times in this book). And if you enjoyed the town of Haven, be sure to check out *An Ex for Christmas* featuring Kelly and Mark Blakely from this book—yes, it's a seasonal book, but it's also a best friends–to-lovers story, which we all know is timeless!

A complete list of my books is available on my website, and be sure to sign up for my newsletter to get notified about the third and final

Man of the Year book, which, as I write this letter, is not yet titled, but I already know features an alpha guy in a suit who I think you guys are going to *love*.

Xo.
Lauren Layne

ACKNOWLEDGMENTS

And now for the list of thank-yous, because we authors *need* our people—I know that I'd be nowhere without mine, especially:

Kristi Yanta, my longtime editor, who never panics, not even when I excitedly handed her the first draft of this book and described it as "a tangled ball of yarn, but a rainbow, glittery tangle!" Thank you for helping me smooth out all those tangles without losing any of the sparkle or vibrancy. You have no idea how much I appreciate you working tirelessly behind the scenes to clean up the messy, hard parts of my manuscripts to get them *just right.*

The Montlake team, especially Maria Gomez, for your support of me and this series. You guys bring your A game to every single cover design, marketing plan, and copyedit, and your attention to detail never, ever goes unappreciated.

Nicole Resciniti, my tireless agent, and Lisa Filipe, my fantastic assistant, for always holding down the Lauren Layne fort while I'm squirreled away in my writer cave.

My author crew, especially Jennifer Probst, Rachel Van Dyken, Jessica Lemmon, and Evie Dumore, for being on the receiving end of many incoherent emails and text messages, and always knowing exactly the right thing to say.

To my friends and family, most especially my husband: you mean so much to me.

To all of my readers: I'm so grateful for you. I've said it before, I'll say it again: thank you for your kindness and your love of romance.

ABOUT THE AUTHOR

Photo © 2019 Anthony LeDonne

Lauren Layne is the *New York Times*, *USA Today*, and Amazon best-selling author of more than thirty novels, including the Man of the Year series and the 21 Wall Street series. Her books have sold more than a million copies and have been translated into multiple languages. Lauren's work has been featured in *O, The Oprah Magazine*; *Publishers Weekly*; *Glamour*; the *Wall Street Journal*; and *Inside Edition*. She is based in New York City, where she's married to her high school sweetheart. For more information visit https://laurenlayne.com.